FADE TO
BLUE

HANK SCHEER

TOP READS PUBLISHING, LLC

Vista, California USA

First Edition

For information about special discounts for bulk purchases, please direct emails to:
info@topreadspublishing.com

Cover design, book layout and typography: Teri Rider & Associates

Printed in the United States of America

Library of Congress Control Number: 2023901319

ISBN: 978-1-970107-34-0 (paperback)
ISBN: 978-1-970107-35-7 (ebook)

Author's note:
This is a work of fiction. Unless otherwise indicated, all the names, characters, businesses, places, events, and incidents in this book are either the product of the author's imagination or used in a fictitious manner. Any resemblance to actual persons, living or dead, or actual events is purely coincidental.

dedication

To Leslie Schwartz

Author. Mentor. Friend. Leslie provided valuable edits and insight. Most important, she convinced me—after much debate—that Sarah should not become a victim of her own creation midway through the book.

preface

———

I had no desire to write a novel and had never written anything of substance—unless you count my annual Christmas cards.

In 1998, I was working as a system repairman at the USS-POSCO steel mill in Pittsburg, California. One evening, a coworker and I were in the break room. She said, "Hey, let's write a short story." I reluctantly agreed.

While bandying about some ideas, I remembered that the KM-CAL line had stopped running because a computer that controls line speed and torque had lost its memory and crashed. I said, "How about this: An evil scientist creates a drug that erases a person's memory."

She decided it would be too difficult for us to write the story together and encouraged me to continue without her. After some hesitation, I jotted down a few ideas.

On January 19, 2023—almost a quarter century after being prodded into writing a short story—I finished *Fade to Blue*.

chapter one

Once again, the pain was too great. Sarah broke her stride and staggered to a halt. She bent over and grasped unsteady knees as her lungs fought for oxygen. She'd stopped smoking just eight months ago and knew it would take time to cleanse the effect of 40,000 cigarettes and regain her stamina. Still, she cursed in frustration that her thirty-two-year-old body couldn't run the entire shoreline of San Gregorio Beach before surrendering.

Sarah remained hunched over for some time, her auburn braids hanging down and moving gently in the breeze. She listened to the crashing of four-foot breakers and watched the foam of spent Pacific waves surge forward and touch the tips of her running shoes before receding.

"Lovely morning."

She jerked her head around and saw an older, well-dressed man standing ten feet behind her.

"Yeah, it is," she said before returning her gaze to the sand.

"We've been lucky. All this sun and no rain."

"Yup."

"I'm curious. Do you run every day or just when the weather is pleasant?"

Sarah rolled her eyes and exhaled derisively.

"You probably take this view for granted. Where I'm from, few people will see an ocean in their lifetime."

She detected an accent and realized he was just a friendly tourist. Breaking an apologetic smile, she turned to face the stranger and was momentarily blinded by the sun. She squinted and observed him while shading her eyes with her right hand. Had she been standing more erect, she would have appeared to be saluting him.

He was a man of average height with a solid build and a full head of dark hair combed back. He wore a charcoal-gray suit and a white turtleneck and was holding a gold-colored shopping bag. Sarah figured him to be about sixty years old. European. And definitely out of place on San Gregorio Beach.

"Where are you from?" she asked.

"A little town in northern Slovakia. But now I live in Paris."

"Lucky you."

"Oh, no. Lucky you," he said. "You get to live in California. Although, I must say, everything here is rather expensive."

"So you noticed."

"Speaking of expensive, may I show you something I

purchased?" he asked, spreading the handles of his Neiman Marcus shopping bag.

Sarah hesitated, then shrugged her shoulders and ambled five steps up to dry sand. She peered into his bag and saw two boxes and a silver-plated handgun with a silencer attached to its barrel. She cocked her head and gave the man an icy stare. "Is that supposed to be a joke?"

"I'm afraid not. The gun is real. And it's loaded. *And* I'm quite proficient with it. So please do as I say. I need—"

"Are you *threatening* me?"

"Sarah." A chill ran up her spine. "I won't harm you. I just need some information."

"How do you know my name?"

"I'll explain everything. But first, you're going to accompany me to those rocks," he said, nodding toward the north end of the beach.

She noticed a young man walking nearby. He was wearing khaki shorts, a tank top that accentuated his muscular upper body, and sunglasses. She bolted over to him and grabbed his shoulders. "Help me. That guy has a gun. He threatened me."

The young man scoffed. "You mean that dude in the suit?"

"Yes. Can you call the police?"

"That's not necessary. He just wants some information. But if you run or scream, he'll blow your fucking head off."

Sarah felt a hand touch her arm and gasped. She whipped around and faced the stranger again.

"Relax, Sarah. We're not going to hurt you."

"Is everything under control?" came a woman's voice from inside his suit jacket.

"I believe so. You and your team just stay put."

Sarah scanned the sparsely populated beach: sunbathers, a family enjoying a picnic lunch, a man reading a book, three teenagers tossing a Frisbee, a woman doing yoga, a couple walking the shoreline with a puppy in tow.

"As you can see, I'm not working alone. Some of the people on this beach are assisting me. Unfortunately, you don't know who is and who isn't. And to tell you the truth, I'm not entirely sure either."

Sarah continued to scrutinize the beachgoers.

"Now, listen carefully. You're going to walk with me to those rocks. Do not scream, run, or draw attention to yourself in any way. Is that clear?"

She took a deep breath. "Look, I don't know who you are or what's going on here. But it's not funny."

"You're right; it's *not* funny. Now come with me. Unless you want to die."

chapter two

*P*anic gripped Sarah as she accompanied the man to his designated spot. With every step, she felt herself sinking deeper into a morass. Overwhelmed by a sense of hopelessness and resigned to her fate, she reluctantly kept pace with him. Stride for stride. Like a condemned prisoner walking to her execution.

They reached the north end of the beach, and the man sat on a sandstone rock formation. He put down his shopping bag and motioned for her to sit next to him. She complied.

He remained silent for an unbearably long ten seconds before speaking. "This did not go as planned. Do you remember those religious canvassers who came to your house this morning?"

Sarah stared ahead and said nothing.

"They were members of my team. Unfortunately, you wouldn't open the door. But then you came to this lovely beach, so we decided to do the intervention here. I think it went quite well."

She suddenly ached to smash his face, and it took every ounce of self-control to keep from delivering an *Empi Uchi*—an elbow strike she'd perfected while earning her black belt. Instead, she vowed that someday she'd watch this oh-so-cultured gentleman being marched out of a courtroom in shackles and an orange jumpsuit. For now, that image would offer solace.

"My name is Marcel," he continued. "Do you know why I contacted you?"

Sarah bristled at his choice of the word "contacted." "Terrorized" would have been more accurate. But she decided not to engage him in a debate over semantics and simply answered his question. "No."

"You mean you have no idea?"

She turned to him. "No, I don't."

"Well then, allow me to explain. I understand you created a brain-destroying drug."

A wave of nausea passed over her, and she silently cursed Paul Johansen. He'd obviously filed a charge against her. So be it. But why not a formal inquiry? Since when did the government use gun-toting thugs to investigate an ethics violation?

She shook her head in disbelief. "Paul told you about T-3, didn't he?"

"T-3? Is that what you call your drug?"

"Yeah. And guess what? He's right. I did an experiment, okay? I'm guilty. I did it because I *fucking* want to find a cure for Alzheimer's."

"I believe you," Marcel said.

"Really? Then why are you treating me like a god-damn terrorist?"

"Are you going to work tomorrow?"

"I don't know. You tell me. Will I make it past security?"

"Of course."

"Is there going to be a hearing?"

"No."

"*No?*" Sarah momentarily closed her eyes. "Wait a minute. I thought this was about an ethics investigation."

Marcel smiled. "We don't care about ethics."

"Then what the hell's going on here?"

"We're interested in your drug. You must write a report detailing its chemical makeup, how it's made, and how it works."

He pulled a business card from his pocket and held it out to her. The words **MEREIN TEST** were embossed on it.

"This is the name you will give the file. Save it to your MEREIN computer desktop before seven thirty tomorrow morning."

She glared at him. "Who *are* you?"

"That's not important."

"No? Well, it's pretty important to *me*."

Marcel glanced at his wristwatch. "I'm sorry, perhaps I should start from the beginning. I have been hired to gain information from you. I will tell you what to do, when to do it, and how to do it. I don't care what you think. You are not an equal partner. And while I won't divulge for whom I work, I will tell you they're quite powerful. And ruthless if need be. So, I would advise you to listen to me and comply with everything you are told. Now, please take this."

Sarah snatched the card from his fingers.

"You have until seven thirty tomorrow morning to post a detailed report. After that, you're going to give us a sample."

He reached inside his gold shopping bag and pulled out a small, white bag with a black stripe around it. "Put a sample of your drug into this bag and keep it in your possession at all times. When I instruct you, you will drive to the McDonald's near your workplace and deposit it into the trash receptacle in the women's toilet."

She gave Marcel a homicidal glare and then looked away. "This is crazy."

"Are you familiar with the restaurant? It's on Alpine Road."

"This is *not* happening."

"Are you familiar with it?"

Sarah snapped back to attention. "Yes. The McDonald's on Alpine Road."

"You will drop off the sample in the women's toilet."

"Sure. Maybe I should flush three times since it's a long way to Paris or wherever the hell you're from."

"No, no. You are to place it into the *trash receptacle* in the women's toilet."

"Over here, we call them 'restrooms.'"

"Do you understand what I want?"

"Oui, oui, Monsieur."

"I trust you have a sample you can supply us."

Sarah had to think before remembering the partially filled vial of T-3 in her desk drawer. "Sorry, I don't have any left. I got rid of it," she lied.

"Then you'll have to produce a new sample before eight o'clock tomorrow morning."

"I can't do that."

"Why?"

"Because someone is bound to ask me what I'm doing. But maybe you don't care."

"You're right. I don't care. You're going to make a T-3 sample and place it in this bag. I will ring you when we're ready for the drop-off."

Marcel placed the white bag on the ground, reached into his Neiman Marcus shopping bag, and removed a flip phone. "This is for you to keep until we've completed our business. When it rings, open the phone and press the green button," he said, pointing to the ON key. Sarah noted his manicured fingernails. "The call will be from me. When we're through talking, press the red one." He pointed to the OFF key. "You see?"

"Yeah, I had a phone like that when I was eleven."

"I won't ring you often. It's primarily a listening device. You'll be monitored twenty-four hours a day."

"What?"

"That's right. You will have to wear this at all times, except when you sleep or are in the shower."

"Wait a minute. You want me to wear that thing so you can eavesdrop on me?"

"Yes."

"That's bullshit."

"You will remove it only for sleeping or showering. And during those times, you must keep it within two meters of your body." He raised the phone close to her face. "This is never to be more than two meters away. Do you understand? Now here—take the phone."

She didn't budge.

"Take it now and attach it to your outfit."

Sarah grudgingly accepted the phone and clipped it to the waistband of her running pants.

Marcel again reached into the shopping bag. "I would like to call your attention to that surfer," he said, nodding toward the ocean. "Don't take your eyes off him."

Sarah saw a young man straddling a surfboard close to shore. She felt Marcel grab her left running shoe and pull up her pant leg. She tried to free her foot, but he held on. "Don't move. And don't look down." He soon removed his grip and sat upright. "I'm done."

Sarah slid up her left pant leg and saw a black and gold ring encircling her ankle.

"It's a global positioning device," he said. "It tells us where you are at all times. And it will trigger an alarm if you are ever more than two meters away from the phone. Do not tamper with it or try to remove it. We will know if you do."

Her heart rate increased, and she again felt nauseous as she grasped the complexity of this shakedown operation. She was clearly outmatched, so her outbursts—however justified—were not doing her much good. At least for now, she'd have to acknowledge their superiority, suppress her anger, and listen carefully to his instructions.

"I know you're an intelligent woman. You're already thinking of ways to get around this. But please beware: We're watching you. We're listening to you. We're monitoring your computers, your phones, Rogelio's phone, your friends' pho—"

"How do you know about Rogelio?"

"We know everything. We're very good at this, so I would strongly advise you not to challenge us. Do you understand?"

She was too shaken to respond.

"*Do you understand?*"

"Yes."

"Good. Because, over the years, I've encountered a few 'clever individuals' in your predicament who believed they could outsmart me. If any of them could speak today, I'm sure they'd advise you against such nonsense. Do not tamper with these devices or try to circumvent them. No swimming or any other activity that would require you to be more than two meters away from the phone. And last, you cannot socialize with anyone until we've completed our business."

Sarah narrowed her eyes on him. "What exactly do you mean by that?"

"Aside from work, you will have no direct contact with anyone."

"But I'm going to a concert tonight."

"No, you're not. And I know your boyfriend is driving home from Southern California on Tuesday. If—"

"Leave Rogelio out of this. He doesn't know any-thing about T-3."

"If you wish Mr. Galvan no harm, you'll stay away from him. Okay?"

She didn't respond.

"Now, it might take my associates a few days to test your T-3 sample and make sure it works. If everything goes according to plan, we should be out of your life by next weekend. And please know that you're being com-pensated. Access your checking account balance when you get home. You'll see what I mean."

Sarah shot him an incredulous look. "You're *pay-ing* me?"

"Money has already been deposited into your bank account. A goodwill gesture in exchange for your coop-eration."

"You think I'm an idiot? If you really did put money into my account, it was to make it look like *I* contacted *you*. Like I made a discovery and offered it for a price."

"No. We believe you should be compensated for your work."

"Well, I don't want your compensation. I don't want any part of this."

"I think I've covered everything. Do you have any questions?"

"*Questions*? I still don't know what's going on here. You—somebody—is trying to extort information from me. You're telling me I have to wear this phone—"

"It's not so complicated," Marcel shot back. "Com-pose a report and save it to your desktop by seven thirty tomorrow morning. When I instruct you, leave a sample of your drug at the McDonald's."

He looked at his watch.

"I cannot stress enough how deadly serious this is. The people who hired me have invested considerable resources to obtain your drug—including hiring a small army to monitor and watch you around the clock. We're very good at this, so you would be foolish to think you can outwit us. Should you try, you will be dealt with heartlessly. And being a woman will buy you no special consideration.

"I wish you no harm, and there will be none if you simply do as instructed. Write the report, leave the sample when I tell you, and do not remove the phone unless you are showering or sleeping. And never allow it more than two meters from your body. Once you fulfill your obligation, we'll disappear, and you'll be left with a substantial amount of money.

"Now, if there is nothing else, I'll leave so you can enjoy the rest of this beautiful day. Just sit still for five minutes before getting up. And don't forget to take the little white bag with you."

He stood. "Remember: we're listening to you twenty-four hours a day. Any time you have a question, say 'Marcel, ring me.' I'll do so immediately."

six months earlier

chapter three

———

Sarah Brenalen flashed her ID card as she drove past the guard shack and into the MEREIN complex. She followed the two-lane road as it snaked alongside a misty pond and through a grove of eucalyptus trees. After passing the gymnasium, tennis courts, and dining commons, she pulled into her assigned parking spot behind the research building.

MEREIN, the Memory Research Institute, was a state-of-the-art facility nestled in Portola Valley, forty miles south of San Francisco. It was the creation of neurologist Neil Obergaard, a world-renowned authority on brain disorders.

The centerpieces of MEREIN were facing glass-encased buildings that from overhead resembled giant boomerangs. Building One was a research center dedicated to solving the mystery of Alzheimer's disease. Building Two was a residence for adults diagnosed with varying degrees of memory loss. It included assisted-living apartments and a nursing home.

Separating these two-story structures was Lincoln Square, an oasis of redwood trees, gardens, sculptures, and water features.

Sarah got out of her car and approached the south entrance to the research building. Two tinted-glass doors slid apart and allowed her to enter. She exchanged greetings with several coworkers while walking down a hallway to a cartoon-plastered door. She unlocked it, entered her office, and flipped the light switch. The wall clock read 8:45 a.m.—fifteen minutes until the Monday morning staff meeting.

Sarah walked into the conference room carrying a mug of coffee and an iPad and flopped down in one of the twenty chairs surrounding the table. Neil Obergaard acknowledged her presence with a nod and continued preparing his notes.

"How was your weekend?" Yuen Li asked.

Sarah turned to the young PhD from Hong Kong. "Great. It was my first one off in a month."

"Did you do anything exciting?"

"Rogelio and I had dinner at Primavera to celebrate our one-year anniversary."

Yuen's face lit up. "Congratulations."

"Thanks. And we also celebrated something else."

"You got engaged?"

"Not yet. *But*—drum roll, please—I've now gone two months without a cigarette."

Yuen flashed an over-the-top look of excitement that quickly morphed into a weary gape. "Thrill."

"Okay, I've quit before. But this time, I'm serious."

"I'd like to get started," Neil announced, prompting all conversations to cease. He picked up a stack of handouts and circulated them around the room. "I'm distributing the nine-month report on the Xanal trial. It details the 1,200 Alzheimer's patients who've been participating, including several of our own residents.

"Some of you helped develop Xanal. And I believe everyone here has been involved one way or another in the study, so it pains me to announce we're terminating the trial."

Audible gasps sounded, and hushed words were exchanged between some staff members. Sarah dropped her head.

"As you know," Neil continued, "this is not a profession for the fainthearted. We endure our share of setbacks. But we carry on because we've devoted our lives to this fight. So, we'll learn what we can from Xanal and press forward."

Sarah left work early. Dejected. It was not the first time. Luckily, she had two things at home to lift her spirits: wine and music. And Rogelio was coming over for dinner. The day would end on a high note.

She parked her Honda Civic in front of the white bungalow she rented from a former Stanford University professor, entered the house, went straight to the refrigerator, and poured herself a glass of Chardonnay.

She left the kitchen and walked into the smaller of her two bedrooms, which she'd converted into a recording studio. Its heart and soul was the workstation—a seven-octave keyboard enhanced with knobs, slide bars, and a user-interface screen. Two wireless speakers and a microphone were mounted above it. To the right was her iMac computer.

Sarah sat down in a swivel chair and turned on the power. The workstation came to life, and her iMac displayed *Music Maker* software. She selected a song titled *All in the Timing*, and the twenty tracks of her latest composition filled the monitor. She'd provided the lead and background vocals for the song and played all the synthesized tracks on her keyboard. She took a sip of wine, clicked PLAY, and heard *All in the Timing's* opening vocal. She increased the volume and sat back in her chair.

At the two-minute mark, she hit STOP, made a few edits, and then resumed the song and listened until it faded out.

"I like it."

She spun around in her chair and saw Rogelio standing in the doorway. "You scared the hell out of me."

"Sorry, I just got here. I didn't want to disturb you."

"It's okay." She got up and walked over to him. They shared a kiss.

"So, how was your day?" he asked.

"Shitty."

"Care to talk about it?"

"No, but you can rewind the tape and listen to our

last discussion about another failed Alzheimer's drug."

"I'm sorry. Here, I brought you a gift," he said and handed her a bottle of massage oil.

She smiled. "Thank you."

"I was going to bring flowers, but this is more fun."

"Oh, yes it is."

"And it'll last longer than flowers."

She gave him a seductive look. "I wouldn't bet on it."

"Hey, can I hear your song from the beginning?"

"Sure. Just promise not to laugh."

Sarah moved the cursor to the start of the song and hit PLAY. She left the room and returned a minute later with a cold bottle of Dos Equis. She handed him the beer and sat in a facing chair.

All in the Timing ended with a lush string chord and a piano embellishment. Rogelio beamed. "It's really good. I think you could get a record deal."

Sarah shook her head. "No way. My songs are okay, but my voice sucks." She leaned forward and stroked his right thigh. "Anyway, have you thought about it?"

"Yeah."

"And?"

He looked at the floor for a moment and then smiled at her. "Let's do it."

Sarah shrieked and wrapped her arms around him. "Are you sure?"

"Yes," he replied before abruptly pulling away from her grasp. "But I want to share a *life* with you—not just a house."

"I agree. I'm going to talk to Neil this week."

"Promise?"

"Yes," Sarah said and held up her wine glass. Rogelio clinked his bottle of beer against it.

"I don't believe it," she exclaimed. "We're going to buy a house."

They discussed several cities they'd consider moving to and narrowed the list down to five. After deciding to give it a rest, Sarah leaned back in her chair and took a sip of wine. Rogelio reached over and picked up a framed photograph of a girl wearing a white karate uniform. She was posed in a fighting stance and had a scowl on her face. "I love this photo."

"Me too."

"When was it taken?"

"The day I got my black belt," Sarah replied. "I was sixteen."

"Wow. Sixteen. And when did you break that guy's jaw?"

"A couple of years later."

Rogelio smirked. "Well, I guess it's nice to know you were able to put all that training to good use."

"Yeah. And hopefully, he learned that 'no' *really does* mean 'no.'" She looked into Rogelio's eyes. "Hey sweetie, you gettin' hungry?"

"Yes. I could definitely eat."

"Okay, then let me rephrase my question: are you absolutely starving right now?"

He laughed. "Okay, then let me rephrase my answer: *no*. Why?"

"Because I'd kinda like to try out that massage oil."

chapter four

———

Sarah was writing a grant proposal when she heard voices. She turned to the open door and saw Neil Obergaard and a middle-aged woman.

"Lauren, I want you to meet Dr. Sarah Brenalen," Neil said. "Sarah, this is Lauren Ross. Her mother, Katherine, has been diagnosed with early-stage Alzheimer's disease and is at the top of the waiting list for one of our assisted-living apartments."

The two women shared a handshake and cordial greetings.

"Lauren's here to fill out some paperwork and get a tour. I was hoping you could show her the labs."

"Sure, I'd be happy to," Sarah said.

"Ms. Ross, I leave you in capable hands. Dr. Brenalen is a pharmacologist and oversees many of our clinical studies. I'm sure you'll get along famously. Now, if you'll both excuse me, I must prepare for an important teleconference." Neil bowed his head and exited the room.

"I know you're busy. I won't take much of your time," Lauren said.

"Please, it's not a problem. I enjoy giving tours."

They left Sarah's office and walked down the hallway. "I'm sorry to hear about your mother. But don't worry, we'll take good care of her."

Sarah stopped at Lab 110 and scanned her ID card. She opened the door, and the two women stepped inside. The room contained an impressive array of scientific equipment and computers. An intern wearing a white lab coat was sitting at one of the six workstations and peering through a microscope.

"This is where we create new Alzheimer's drugs," Sarah said to Lauren in a hushed voice. "If they get approved by the FDA, we produce research-grade compounds for testing mice."

They left Lab 110, walked down the hall to Lab 114, and donned disposable white suits and booties. Sarah led her guest into a sterilized room lined with cages, each containing a dozen or so rodents. A combination of faint bleach and sawdust permeated the air.

"These are our special mice," Sarah said. "Each one has a microchip implanted just beneath the skin of its neck. We can scan any one of them with a hand-held communicator and get all its relevant information—age, sex, diet, regimens."

"Interesting," Lauren said.

"All of these mice were born with a dormant model of the Alzheimer's gene. We train them through a process called 'food-light association' and let them reach a relatively old age before activating the gene. Then we include them in drug studies.

"For example, I'm heading up a study involving 160 mice. We triggered their Alzheimer's gene and began giving half of them a new drug called Prelozen. The others are receiving a placebo. Over the next few months, we'll document the progression of Alzheimer's and the relative effectiveness of the drug."

Sarah noticed Lauren staring off into space. "I'm sorry, is this too much information?"

"No, not at all," she responded. "But I'm struck by the fact that you have all this sophisticated equipment and technology, yet it seems we're no closer to understanding Alzheimer's disease than we were ten years ago."

"That's not true," Sarah said. "We've actually learned a lot."

"But we're still a long way from a cure."

"Not necessarily. I'm optimistic there could soon be an effective drug."

Lauren offered a wistful smile. "Soon enough to help my mother?"

"That's my hope," Sarah replied, even though she knew the right answer was no.

———

Sarah and her best friend, Dr. Margaret Owens, carried their lunch trays over to a table in the MEREIN cafeteria and sat down. Margaret, her hair arranged in shoulder-length cornrows and wearing a green blouse and black dress pants, tasted her tomato soup and reached for the saltshaker. "So, you and Rogelio are buying a house?"

"Yes," Sarah replied as she drizzled vinaigrette on her salad. "Rents are getting ridiculous. And besides, we want to live together. Unfortunately, our schedules aren't in sync."

"Meaning?" Margaret asked while adding a considerable amount of salt to her soup.

"He starts work at six in the morning."

"Ouch."

"I know. Which means he's getting ready for bed by the time I get home."

Margaret narrowed her eyebrows. "Doesn't that kind of defeat the purpose of living together?"

"It's a bummer, but we'll figure it out. And, we do have weekends together."

"You mean the ones you're not working?"

Sarah frowned. "Yeah."

Over lunch they discussed grueling work schedules, failed drug trials, and Sarah's unorthodox theory for an Alzheimer's cure that Neil had rebuffed.

Sarah eventually checked her watch. "Oh shit, I gotta run." They bussed their trays and walked back to Building One. Margaret returned to Lab 110, where she was analyzing brain samples of recently deceased Alzheimer's patients. Sarah entered Neil's office and sat down on a sepia leather couch that faced his desk. He was reclining in his captain's chair, hands clasped and resting on his stomach.

"I trust you're bringing good news."

"I wish," Sarah said. "Yuen and I just finished another round of tests. Nine percent of the Prelozen mice failed food-light."

Neil jerked forward. "Are you serious?"

"Yup. And stupid me. I thought Prelozen was going to be a breakthrough."

"Let's not concede defeat just yet. We're still in the early stages of this trial."

"I agree," she acknowledged. "But I'm not holding my breath."

He picked up a pen and scribbled unreadable words on a notepad. "You need to give a report to the next staff meeting."

"Oh, boy. I can't wait."

Neil set the pen down and looked at her. "Your frustration is palpable."

"Ya think?"

He leaned back and rocked in his chair. "If it's any consolation, when I first envisioned MEREIN, I promised potential donors we'd have an Alzheimer's cure by the end of the millennium if we built this facility."

Sarah slowly nodded her head. "Well, we still have a shot."

"That was in 1989."

"Oh. In that case, we failed miserably."

"Yes," Neil acknowledged with a weary smile. "I suppose we have."

Sarah inhaled and exhaled a deep breath. "I want to test my theory."

"No. We've already discussed this."

"I have a sample of LDMR."

"So what? You can't strengthen a brain by attacking it."

"How do you know?" Sarah said. "The brain might defend itself and become more resilient."

"A brain is *incapable* of defending itself."

"So we were taught in Neuroscience 101. But what if that's not true? The human brain is the most sophisticated organ that's ever existed. And frankly, we know very little about it. All I'm asking is one experiment. Just one."

"No. Now please drop it."

"Fine." Sarah stood, took four steps toward the door, and did an about-face. "And another thing. I need weekends off. I want to spend more time with Rogelio."

Neil pressed forward again. "Don't you think I'd like more time with *my* family?"

"I've been working sixty hours a week."

"So has everyone else. We sacrifice personal aspirations for the advancement of humanity. You knew that when you signed on."

"Yes, but I still want a life. I'm tired of coming in here every weekend. And I'm tired of pinning my hopes on some new drug, only to discover it holds no more promise than the last one."

Neil lowered his head and then looked back at her. "I'll do what I can to cut back on your hours. But it's unrealistic to think you're going to have every weekend off."

"Then maybe I should get another job."

"Doing what?"

She pondered his question. "I've thought about becoming an electrical engineer."

Neil exhaled loudly. "You'd walk away from the most pressing medical challenge of the twenty-first century to become a dime-a-dozen electrical engineer?"

"I don't know. It's a thought."

Neither spoke as they processed their discussion. Neil finally broke the silence. "Wasn't your father an electrical engineer?"

"No. He was an electrician."

"Aah, yes. And if memory serves me, he taught you the trade."

"Not exactly. But he *did* teach me Ohm's law. And he brought home a bunch of electrical gadgets for me to take apart and play with."

Neil smiled. "So instead of Barbie dolls, you played with motors and transistors."

"Yeah. We even started building a robot together. Then he died."

His smile disappeared. "I'm sorry. If I may ask. . . ."

"He was killed by an arc flash."

"And now you want a job in that same profession?"

Sarah shook her head. "No way. But I could be an engineer."

"Well," Neil said, "I'm sure you'd make a fine electrical engineer. But I have the utmost respect for you and your work, and I don't want to lose you."

chapter five

The fire caused little damage, and no one was injured. Nonetheless, Kendrick Perkins had committed his third infraction in less than a month.

Taking note of that fact, the seven members of the MEREIN Housing Review Board wrote a report expressing their collective opinion that Mr. Perkins should surrender his assisted-living apartment for a more closely monitored room in the nursing home.

Sarah sipped coffee as she read the board's report. Perkins had been frying a steak on the kitchen stove when he inexplicably left his apartment to go for a walk. Sometime later, a nurse heard a screeching smoke detector, gained entry to his apartment, and extinguished a small fire.

Perkins's decline was a huge blow. He'd moved into MEREIN after being diagnosed with mild Alzheimer's symptoms and functioned well for a couple of years. A physicist by profession, his science lectures were a hit with residents and staff alike. He was also an accomplished pianist and performed regularly on the grand piano in the dining room foyer. But MEREIN's most beloved resident was now failing, his brain ceding to the scourge of Alzheimer's.

Sarah finished reading the report and closed her eyes. Devastated by the mental deterioration of her friend, she again contemplated her provocative "strengthen the brain by attacking it" theory that Neil had refused to consider. In fairness, she knew that until recently her theory couldn't be tested because the blood-brain barrier would prevent toxic drugs from entering. But now, there was LDMR—a Trojan horse. By fusing synapse-attacking drugs to LDMR, the blood-brain barrier would allow them to enter.

She had an LDMR sample in her desk drawer and had designed three synapse-targeting compounds. Why not conduct a secret experiment? What was there to lose? If the result confirmed Neil was right, she might throw in the towel and pursue another career. However, if her experiment showed promise, it could provide the jolt of inspiration she needed to stay the course and fight for her theory.

Sarah waited in her office until everyone else had gone home for the day. She removed the little vial of LDMR from her desk drawer and walked down the hallway to Lab 110. She turned on lights and equipment, opened a refrigerator filled with drugs, and selected the ones she wanted for her tests.

She produced a .1-milliliter amount of a new compound, fused it to LDMR, and diluted it in sterile saline. She drew a sample of her new drug into a syringe and deposited the rest into a vacuum-sealed vial for possible use later. Using various compounds, she repeated that process twice and created three new Alzheimer's drugs in less than an hour.

Sarah left Lab 110 with the syringes and vials stuffed in her lab coat pockets and entered Lab 114, the "rodent room." She removed a mouse from a cage and scanned it with her hand-held communicator. Number 319078. She jotted down its number on a notepad, and next to it "T-1" for test drug number one. She injected the mouse with half of the first syringe, placed it back inside the cage, grabbed a second mouse, wrote down its number, and injected it with the remaining T-1.

She worked quickly and methodically, injecting a total of six mice with her three drugs. Just like that, the experiment was done. She cleaned up and walked out of Building One, feeling a mixture of anxiety, excitement, and shame.

Sarah thought about her illicit experiment on the drive home. She'd just violated the medical code of ethics, and it weighed heavily on her conscience. In addition, testing three new concoctions on six mice could hardly be considered a scientific study. But it was imperative that the quantity of drugs she'd used be inconsequential to go undetected. Besides, she was just hoping for a sign. Her drugs had now slipped past the blood-brain barrier of the six mice. If one or more of them fared surprisingly well in a future drug study, perhaps she was on to something.

———

Sarah stiffened when Gaitri Singh reported to the staff meeting that she'd quarantined two unresponsive and potentially diseased mice. She approached Gaitri after the meeting and expressed concern.

The twenty-three-year-old intern from Mumbai led Sarah to a cage containing the two mice in question. She scanned both with a communicator and saved their numbers. "Thank you. I'll take it from here," she assured Gaitri.

Sarah returned to her office and opened the notepad documenting her experiment. Her heart thumped. The numbers on the communicator's screen matched the two mice she'd injected with T-3.

T-3 contained an active fragment of an astrocyte proliferation cytokine, plus sub-lethal doses of calcium and glucocorticoid. She'd hoped this combination would impel the brain to boost glucose metabolism and fortify neural transmissions. But far from strengthening the brain, her drug had apparently done the opposite.

She monitored the listless mice for several hours. They didn't move and were unresponsive to offerings of food and water. She decided to administer a Positron Emission Tomography (PET) scan on one of them.

Sarah clipped on her dosimeter badge and brought one of the mice to Lab 131. She injected a radioactive tracer into its tail vein and placed it on a disposable sheet under the scanner. She grimaced when a rendering of the mouse's brain appeared on the screen. It was almost entirely blue in color, meaning no neural activity. Only the brain stem was functioning. It radiated warm splashes of orange and red, signifying that this hard-wired region was still regulating heart rate, respiration, and body temperature. But it was all for naught. The mouse was essentially brain-dead.

Sarah took deep breaths in an unsuccessful attempt to calm her racing heart. She carried the mouse back to her office and tried to come to grips with what she'd just seen. Had her T-3 caused this damage, or had both mice been stricken by something unrelated to her experiment? After much soul searching, she felt compelled to perform another test.

Sarah brought a mouse to Lab 131, injected it with a radioactive tracer combined with an anesthetic, and administered a PET scan. On the monitor, she saw the red-orange-yellow-green spectrum of a typical brain. As the mouse lay sedated under the scanner, she took the syringe of T-3, poked the needle into its tail vein, and squeezed the plunger. Within a minute, most of the red, orange, yellow, and green regions of its brain had faded to blue. Even the cortex, which is resilient to many drugs, was blue.

The only exception—once again—was the brain stem, which continued to regulate the most basic, life-supporting functions. She sat motionless, in shock and disbelief.

With deep remorse, Sarah euthanized the three debilitated mice. "I decided to err on the side of caution," she later told Neil and Gaitri.

For several days, Sarah monitored the mice in Lab 114. Those she'd injected with T-1 and T-2 showed no ill effects and lived normally within the general population. T-3, on the other hand, had proved to be a bombshell, and she desperately wanted to talk to someone about it. But who? Certainly not Neil or anyone else at MEREIN.

The answer came one evening while making dinner. "Paul," she whispered to herself. Yes, she would confess her sins to Paul Johansen, the brilliant neuroscientist who'd worked at MEREIN before moving to New York to accept a position at the NYU School of Medicine. Since she'd conducted her experiment with the best of intentions, he'd hopefully condone her undisciplined behavior. And most important, Paul was a genius. He'd comprehend the chemical makeup of T-3 and would be able to explain how an infinitesimal amount of her creation could destroy a brain in sixty seconds.

Sarah went to her studio, sat at the computer, and Googled NYU School of Medicine. She clicked on its website and did a faculty search for Paul Johansen. A page opened with his photo and biography. His contact information included a phone number and email address. She called the number and left a message urging him to call her back.

———

Sarah was writing an email when her office phone rang. She noticed the New York City area code and picked up the receiver.

"Paul. Long time. How are you?"

"I'm doing well. And you?"

"Hangin' in there," Sarah replied. "You got a few minutes?"

"Yes."

She closed the office door and emptied her soul to him: her frustration over the slow progress in finding an Alzheimer's cure, the fatigue from six-day workweeks, and her growing inclination to leave MEREIN and start a new career.

"Wow," Paul said. "That's a lot to digest."

"Wait. I haven't even gotten to the shocker yet."

She then explained her theory, her experiment, and the horrifying result of T-3.

"I don't believe it. Please tell me you're joking."

"I'm not. Everything I just told you is true."

"Sarah! No! How could you even *think* about doing something like that?"

"I wanted to see if—"

"And why are you telling *me*?"

"Because you're the smartest person I know."

"Gee, thanks. Now I have to file an ethics violation charge against you."

She scoffed. "Oh, come on, Paul."

"If you know someone has committed an ethics violation, you're obligated to report it."

It suddenly occurred to her that during Paul's tenure at MEREIN, she'd spurned his romantic advances. "This isn't about us, is it?

"What? No, of course not. But if I do nothing and the truth comes out, I'm just as liable."

"No one else knows about this. Let's keep it that way. Okay?"

He didn't respond.

"Paul, please. Hear me out. I injected four mice with two other drugs I designed. Give me a chance to see how they do. Okay? I just need some time."

She heard him exhale into the phone. "I don't know. Let me think about it."

With that, he ended the call.

Sarah held the receiver for a moment and then set it on the cradle. For a few minutes, she sat at her desk, head in hands.

———

Paul Johansen hung up the phone and shook his head in disbelief. "Dammit. How could you do that?" he whispered.

He recounted the first time he met Sarah. It was just after he'd started working at MEREIN. Neil Obergaard introduced them, and he was immediately smitten. A few weeks later, after learning she was single, he gained the confidence to ask her out for dinner. She politely declined. His anxiety turned to heartache. And humiliation. If only she'd said yes. If only she'd given him a chance.

Regardless, her rejection of a dinner date years ago did not influence his decision. Not one bit. She'd broken the rules and had to be held accountable.

He got up from his chair and retrieved a folder full of reports and notes he'd collected at a recent conference. He laid the folder on his desk and paged through its contents until he found a report titled "Ethical Questions in the Globalization of Medicine." Stapled to the first page was a business card for an ethics committee.

He sat at his computer and composed an email.

To Whom It May Concern:

I'm writing to inform you of a major ethics violation.

Sarah Brenalen, a former colleague of mine, told me she conducted illicit experiments at the Memory Research Institute (MEREIN) with the intent of finding an Alzheimer's cure. In doing so, she accidentally created a drug that—in a concentration as low as a few parts per million— immediately destroys almost all brain functions. (Note: to my knowledge, no such substance has heretofore existed.)

I believe this matter requires your resolute attention—and not only because her actions constitute a gross violation of protocol. Assuming she's right (and I have no reason to doubt her), this drug could pose a serious threat to the public if it gets into the wrong hands.

Please feel free to contact me.
Sincerely,
Paul Johansen, PhD
New York University School of Medicine

Paul read his letter and reaffirmed that he could not stay silent, regardless of how she took it. He moved the cursor to the top of the screen and clicked "Send."

the present

chapter six

———

Sarah sat motionless at San Gregorio Beach, shaken by the invasion into her life. She wanted to believe this was a prank—Paul just trying to scare the crap out of her and teach her a lesson. If so, he'd made his point. Lesson learned. All would be forgiven if Paul, Marcel, and the supporting cast joined hands and took a collective bow.

But this was no prank. This was a living nightmare, triggered by her undisciplined actions. And the nightmare was only going to get scarier. Unknown, dangerous people would soon have a sample of her brain-destroying creation. She'd imagined that as a possibility when she conducted her experiment.

Fearing a panic attack coming on, she sat upright, took several deep breaths, and watched a cargo ship proceed at a snail's pace toward the horizon. As her heart rate returned to somewhat normal, she shifted her eyes to the beach.

A family of four, lugging cabana chairs, a cooler, and a picnic basket, had just arrived and were staking out a prime spot. Additional sunbathers and their blankets now dotted the sand. Twenty or so people walked the shoreline. Everyone seemed to be enjoying this warm, sunny day at the beach. She'd been enjoying her day as well, until a confrontation with terrorists turned her world upside down. Now they were gone, and she sat alone with her GPS anklet, eavesdropping flip phone, and a little white bag with a black stripe.

Sarah got up from the rock and walked a long stretch of sand and a short stretch of asphalt to her car. She retrieved her iPhone from the glove compartment, called Margaret, and explained that she wouldn't be able to go to the concert. "I'm really sorry, but something came up. You guys have a great time."

She drove out of the beach parking lot and got onto Highway 84, heading east. While navigating the winding road, she checked the rearview mirror several times for any sign of vehicles. No one was following her.

A few miles inland from the Pacific Ocean, she started the long climb. Farms and ranches gave way to rolling hills that, in turn, graduated into the Santa Cruz Mountains. Highway 84 finally reached its apex—a vantage point that offered spectacular views of San Francisco Bay—and began its descent. The lush forest of the mountains thinned with the drop in elevation and disappeared altogether as she returned to sea level and civilization. A sign welcomed drivers to Redwood City, population 81,643.

Sarah enjoyed living here. It was close to work, conveniently located between San Francisco and San Jose, and just ninety minutes from wine country. Double that if she was driving to a ski resort at Lake Tahoe.

She spotted a Quick Mart and pulled into the parking lot. After a minute of introspection, she got out of her car, walked inside the store, and approached a man standing behind the counter.

"A pack of Marlboro Lights, please."

With a guilty conscience, she completed the transaction and drove home. She entered her house, strode into the bathroom, pulled down her running pants, and sat on the toilet. Marcel's flip phone dangled near the floor. She stared at it and, for the first time, grasped the implications of the insidious little eavesdropping device.

This is bullshit.

She stood, reached over to the sink, and turned both faucets on full blast.

———

Sarah went from room to room, closing shades while simultaneously turning on inside lights to compensate for the loss of sun. When the last shade was drawn, she covered the camera lens on her computer and flip phone with electrical tape, and inspected walls, furniture, appliances, bookcases, potted plants, and artwork for hidden cameras.

Confident that Marcel hadn't installed visual surveillance, she walked to the bathroom, set the phone on the vanity, and got undressed.

After taking a shower, she put on a pair of blue sweatpants and a matching top and made a cup of coffee. She carried her coffee into the dining room, set it next to her cigarettes and ashtray on an oak table, and grabbed two sheets of paper and a pen from the studio before returning to the dining room and taking a seat at the table on one of four hardwood chairs.

She lit her first cigarette in eight months, took a sip of coffee, and began documenting everything about her ordeal:

> *Accosted by a man named Marcel at*
> *San Gregorio Beach*
> *60ish   5'10"   180-200 pounds*
> *Dark hair*
> *Stylishly dressed*
> *Spoke with an accent*

She continued writing and penned line after line of detailed notes that included such seemingly insignificant observations as the color of Marcel's shoes and the quality of his fingernails. Occasionally she closed her eyes and replayed a segment of the day's events before committing it to ink.

In less than fifteen minutes, she wrote two pages of recollections. After reviewing them and deciding there were no serious omissions, she leaned back in her chair and stared at the ceiling. She mentally dissected everything Marcel had told her during their encounter: the small army assigned to watch her, the two-meter rule, the eavesdropping phone. Was all of it true, or did he weave a fair amount of fiction into his narrative? Driving home from the beach, she'd pondered this question and decided it would be too dangerous to challenge his claims. But now, her curiosity and rebellious nature were conspiring to overturn that decision. It was time for an experiment.

Sarah took two last drags off her cigarette and extinguished it. She unclipped the phone from her sweats and set it down on the table. She stood, moved around her chair, and stepped backward. After pausing, she took another step. And another. The flip phone was now at least two meters away, and she waited nervously for something to happen.

Nothing did.

With her eyes riveted on the phone, she inched backward until her heels touched the wall. She could hear the ticking of her antique clock from its perch on the fireplace mantle in the living room. Its cadence was all that disturbed an otherwise eerie silence. A minute passed. There was no phone call. No audible alarm. No commandos rappelling from black helicopters.

Gaining confidence, she walked a circuitous route through the house before returning to the dining room. Standing in the doorway, she again observed the phone and waited.

Nothing happened.

She began to relax and even managed a cunning smile.

Oh, yoo-hoo! Inspector Clouseau. I just violated your sacred radius of death. What are you going to do about it?

She sat down at the table, penned *Two-meter rule is bogus*, and underlined *bogus* twice.

The flip phone rang, and the unexpected noise startled her. It rang again, and she answered the call.

"Hello?"

"Were you testing me?"

"Marcel?"

"Didn't we discuss the two-meter rule?"

"Yes."

"Then can you explain why you just violated it?"

Her heart raced. "What? I wasn't aware that I had."

"Well, you did."

"I guess . . . uh . . . I was changing clothes . . ."

"And?"

"It won't happen again."

"That's what I wanted to hear. Goodbye."

She put down the phone, feeling like an overconfident chess player who'd just heard the word "checkmate." She lit another cigarette and took a puff. The eerie ringtone sounded again.

"Hello?"

"I just want to reaffirm that we're not going to harm you. Follow my instructions, and we will soon be out of your life. Do you understand?"

"Yes."

"There's no reason to be nervous."

"I'm not nervous."

"Are you sure about that?"

"Yes. Why?"

"How many cigarettes did you smoke last week?"

"I don't know . . . none."

"And you're now smoking your second one in fifteen minutes. To me, that's a mark of someone who's nervous. Are you plotting something?"

"No," she blurted out.

"Then there's no reason to be nervous. Just do what I asked of you. And keep the phone within two meters of your body—as you did in the shower. Goodbye, Sarah."

Her back tingled, as if hundreds of ants were running across it. She sat perfectly still, her mouth slightly open. The clock pendulum ticked eighteen times before she lowered the phone from her ear, pressed the OFF button, and set it on the table.

In her painstaking inspection of the house, she'd found no evidence of visual surveillance. But the flip phone was certainly a powerful listening device. Marcel had heard the faint sounds of her cigarette smoking and could probably hear everything else. Her respiration. Heartbeat. The most intimate sounds from her life.

This was such a cruel violation of her privacy, made even more odious by the fact that he was enjoying it. She imagined him surrounded by high-tech equipment and sporting a lecherous grin. He was toying with her. Humiliating her. And there was nothing she could do about it.

She let out a shriek and pounded her fists on the table with such force that the phone jumped. She pounded again, and then a third time, accentuating each with a guttural release. Hopefully, her outbursts had fractured his eardrums. She wanted to take the phone, run outside, throw it high into the air, and watch it descend and shatter on the sidewalk.

Instead, she pledged to get revenge. But now, the image of Marcel being led away in an orange jumpsuit and shackles no longer provided satisfaction. She wanted to kill him.

———

The closing credits scrolled rapidly up her sixty-inch television screen, and would have made for a good speed-reading exercise, except that the words were in Italian.

Sarah had hoped to enjoy a brief respite from her ordeal by watching a movie while eating dinner. And indeed, *La Finestra* transported her to Rome, where she met Stefania and Roberto and followed their passionate yet turbulent relationship that seemed so appropriate for a young Italian couple. But her immersion into *la dolce vita* was frequently interrupted by mental images of Marcel and flashbacks to their beach encounter.

And now, her escape to the Eternal City was officially over, and she was back in Redwood City. As she turned off the television, the lingering images of cobblestone walkways and magnificent fountains faded, and Marcel again haunted her. His stare. His threats. His bone-chilling voice that under normal circumstances might be soothing to her ears. She picked up her dinner plate, silverware, and empty wine glass and carried them into the kitchen.

Raucous barking shattered the evening quiet, and

Sarah froze. Semba and Spyke, Rottweilers owned by a man living on Clinton Court, had become agitated and were letting the world know about it. She turned off the kitchen light, parted a shade, and peered out the window onto her backyard. As the dogs intensified their blood-curdling racket, her unblinking eyes adjusted to the darkness, and she could make out her deck, her lemon tree, and a swath of lawn. Nothing out of the ordinary. Nothing that didn't belong. The Rottweilers eventually stopped barking, and she was left to wonder what had triggered their wrath.

Sarah kept the light off while cleaning the kitchen. By the time she finished wiping down the counters, she had a plan. She'd go into work early and write the T-3 report. After the Monday morning staff meeting, she'd walk to the gymnasium and enter the women's locker room. A water aerobics class and other activities would be underway, meaning that many lockers would contain clothes and other personal items. Since most of them would be unlocked—few people worried about theft at MEREIN—she could go down the line opening them until she found a phone. She'd borrow it and text the FBI. They'd have time to stake out the McDonald's before Marcel instructed her to do the drop. It seemed like a perfect plan. After all, there was no way he was monitoring *every* resident and staff member.

Then she considered a bold idea: why not leave a harmless drug at McDonald's? If things went according to plan, Marcel would be in handcuffs before he could test the sample. However, there was one potential problem: what if he got away? He'd discover she tricked him. It was not worth the risk. She'd leave a genuine T-3 sample and trust that the Feds would take him down.

She began composing in her mind the text message she'd send to the FBI when her iPhone rang. The name Rogelio Galvan appeared on its screen.

"Shit," she uttered and answered his call.

"Hey, babe. How's it going?" he asked.

"Great. And you?"

"It's all good, except that I miss you."

"I miss you too," Sarah said.

"Hey, so here's an idea. I'm coming home Tuesday. I should be in your neck of the woods around seven. How about I treat you to dinner?"

Her heart rate quickened. "That sounds wonderful, but I'm going to be tied up all week. I'm writing an article for a medical journal."

"Well, congratulations."

"Thanks. It's my first time getting published, and I'm a little stressed out."

"No doubt. So, are you working Saturday?"

"No," she replied. "Neil gave me the weekend off."

"Then let's do dinner Friday night. And some house hunting on Saturday."

"Sure."

"Great. I can't wait to see you. Love you, babe."

"I love you too. Goodnight," she said and ended the call.

Sarah poured herself another glass of Chardonnay and took a sip. She hadn't seen Rogelio in over a week and ached to wrap her arms around him. But first, there was some business to complete. Hopefully, it would be completed by Friday.

She took another sip of wine, closed her eyes, and thought back on the events at the beach. Suddenly it hit her. Marcel said they'd deposited money into her checking account. She'd somehow overlooked that rather important fact while scribing her notes.

She walked over to her computer, opened Bank of America's website, and entered her username and passcode. Her account home page appeared on the monitor. She saw the amount and gasped. It couldn't be real. But there it was. *Her* bank. *Her* home page. To the right of the words "Classic Interest Checking Account" and below the word "Balance" she saw $1,012,862.57.

chapter seven

Sarah encountered little traffic on Woodside Road. It was instead a thick fog that slowed her progress. Visibility was limited, and driving with her face closer to the windshield didn't seem to help. The temperature inside her car had not yet risen above forty degrees, so the cup of coffee she clutched in her right hand provided a welcome, if meager, source of heat. She sipped it and exhaled a translucent cloud.

Her murky view revealed closed businesses and deserted sidewalks. Even Mel's Diner, which advertised an "Early Bird Breakfast Special," was dark. The numerals on her dashboard clock read 5:17.

Sarah accelerated up the entrance ramp to Highway 280 and merged into a plodding procession of diffused headlights. She exited at Alpine Road, drove a quarter mile, and turned onto MEREIN Drive, leaving behind the relative security of other commuters.

MEREIN first appeared as a muted glow in the distance. She reached the guard shack, and the security guy working graveyard shift raised a curious eyebrow at her early arrival.

She parked her car, walked across the otherwise empty lot into Building One, and was immediately assaulted by fluorescent light. She passed a janitor pushing a cleaning cart, and they exchanged smiles. Inside her office, she brewed a pot of coffee. There was much work to do.

Antoine Boucher cursed the cold and fog as he walked the sidewalk in Redwood City. His leather jacket, which held a flashlight in one pocket and a handgun in the other, provided little protection from frigid gusts of wind. Nearing his destination, he looked over his shoulder to make sure he wasn't being followed, and then turned onto a flagstone walkway that brought him to a one-story house.

He pulled out his flashlight, shined its beam on the front door lock and, after a few attempts, managed to insert a key. He unlocked the door, opened it, and stepped inside.

"It's just me," Antoine called out.

He locked the door behind him, rubbed his hands together, and entered the command center. The wall clock read 5:07 a.m. "Sorry I'm late," he said to Erika DuBois. "It's foggy as hell outside."

The young woman pivoted away from the computer screen and looked up at her relief. "I didn't know hell was foggy."

Antoine walked to the coffee maker, which sat on a card table in a corner of the room and poured the dregs of the pot into a Styrofoam cup. "Anything to report?"

"Sarah set off a Transmitter 1 alarm yesterday afternoon."

"The two-meter thing?"

"Yeah. Right after she got home from the beach. She might have been challenging us. Who knows? Marcel called her and explained the rules again."

"Anything else?"

Erika shrugged. "She watched a movie and talked to her boyfriend. Went to bed around ten. It's been quiet all night. Everything's documented in the logbook."

Antoine emptied two sugar packets into his coffee. "So tell me: did you have a hard time staying awake all night listening to her snoring?"

She laughed. "Yes. The 'Sarah snoozer' was definitely a challenge."

"Then you must be tired. Why don't you take off? I got it covered."

"Thanks," Erika said. "Oh, by the way. We only have one video input." She pointed to a monitor that displayed an infrared image of Sarah's house. FRONT VIEW was written in block letters across the top. "Still no luck with the other camera."

"Why?"

"We tried a few times to install one, but it's not easy getting to her backyard. There's another house and fences in the way. And the dogs go crazy every time we show up."

"Why don't we poison them?"

"Because poisoning dogs is a crime. Marcel doesn't want cops snooping around, knocking on doors, asking questions. It's the last thing we need."

"So, how does he—"

"Hold on," Erika said. She turned away from Antoine and listened to sounds coming from a pair of desk speakers. "I think Sarah is leaving her house."

"At five in the morning?"

"She's probably going to work. Marcel wants her report in a couple of hours."

A series of beeps coming from another computer monitor caught Erika's attention. She spun in her chair and brought up an Alarm screen. TRANSMITTER 2 ALARM appeared in bright red letters. She clicked the ACKNOWLEDGE box to silence the disturbance and picked up a push-to-talk phone from the desk.

"Sam: Is there a problem?"

"Yeah, it's freezing out here."

"Okay. Other than frostbite?"

"Not that I'm aware of. We're following Sarah down Woodside. Why do you ask?"

"Never mind," Erika said and put down the phone. She studied a couple of screens on her computer monitor and offered an expletive.

Antoine carried his cup of coffee to the workstation and peered over her shoulder. "What's wrong?"

"Marcel put two trackers on Sarah," Erika replied. She opened a screen that displayed a map of Redwood City. TRANSMITTER 1 was written across the top. She pointed to a flashing white dot near the center of the map. "That dot shows the location of the anklet Sarah's wearing. Right now, it's on Woodside Road."

She then switched to the TRANSMITTER 2 screen, which featured a similar map and flashing dot. "This dot shows the location of the Smart Pebble Marcel attached to her running shoe. As you can see, it's still inside her house. The phone is sending us an alarm because the Smart Pebble is more than thirty meters away."

"What's the purpose of that second GPS?" Antoine asked.

"It's a backup. Let's say Sarah is able to remove the anklet. She could leave it next to the cell phone and escape. We wouldn't know unless we get a motion alarm, or one of the surveillance guys sees her. But if she escapes wearing the shoe with the Smart Pebble, the phone will send us an alarm when she's thirty meters away."

Antoine nodded. "Got it."

"But there's one problem. Sarah's wearing a different pair of shoes than she wore at the beach, so the alarm won't go away until she gets home."

Erika looked up at Antoine. "I'll keep this alarm silenced for now. Unless you want to hear those annoying beeps all day."

———

Sarah was editing the T-3 report she'd written for Marcel when a voice interrupted her concentration: "What are you doing here so early?"

She spun in her chair and saw Margaret standing in her office doorway. She grabbed the mouse and clicked the minimize option. Her report disappeared from the screen.

Margaret laughed. "Oh, come on. I wasn't going to read your love letter to Rogelio. I noticed your door was open and thought, *That can't be Sarah. It's not even eight o'clock.*"

"I had some things to catch up on, so I came in early. But more important, how was Jazz in the Park?"

"Awesome. Great music, food, wine. What can I say? You missed out, girl."

Sarah frowned. "Sorry, I had a lot going on."

"No worries. There's always next time. Anyway, I'll let you go back to work," Margaret said and walked away.

Sarah maximized her four-page report, read it over, and made a few final edits. It was accurate—and intentionally packed with so many formulas that Neil Obergaard would struggle to make sense of it. She saved the report as MEREIN TEST to her desktop as Marcel had instructed.

She unlocked her desk drawer, pulled out the vial of T-3, and saw that it was two-thirds full. She drew several milliliters of the drug into a syringe, injected it into another vial, and put it inside the little white bag Marcel had given her.

Sarah left Building One after the staff meeting and walked a stone path through Lincoln Square toward the gymnasium—hopefully to a phone she could borrow. With each step, she mentally refined her text message to the FBI. Most important: do not arrest the woman who retrieves the T-3 sample. She's just a courier. Follow her when she leaves the McDonald's.

Midway through Lincoln Square, Sarah stopped in her tracks and silently cursed. There was a flaw in her plan. Almost every phone manufactured in the past ten years requires facial recognition or a four-digit passcode. *You can't just borrow someone's phone.* How could she have missed that little detail?

In search of ideas, she continued walking and soon thought of something that gave her reason for optimism. Many of MEREIN's residents were intimidated by anything new in their lives and clung to their old, familiar possessions. It was possible that one or more of the women participating in the water aerobics class still had a not-so-smart phone.

She reached the gymnasium and had just opened the front door when Marcel called.

"We uploaded your report," he said. "Do you have the drug sample?"

"Yes."

"Good. I need you to drive home."

"Why?"

"You'll find out. Go to your car and put the phone on speaker mode so we can talk."

"I have to get something from my locker first."

"No."

"It's a medication I need."

"Go to your car *now*."

Sarah reluctantly changed course, walked to the Building One parking lot, and got into her Honda Civic. She put the flip phone on the passenger seat, started the engine, and drove out of the MEREIN complex. Three minutes later, she came to a stop at Alpine Road.

"Sarah, can you hear me?" Marcel asked.

"Yes."

"Get on Highway 280 heading south."

"But . . . I thought I was driving home."

"No, you're not."

Sarah took the entrance ramp, merged onto a southbound lane of Highway 280, and drove a few miles before hearing his voice again. "Take the next exit."

Sarah flipped her turn signal, got off the freeway, and came to a stop at the end of the ramp.

"Get back on the highway. This time I want you to go north."

"Why?"

"Just do it."

Sarah took a left and drove past the entrance ramp.

"Shit."

"I told you to—"

"I didn't see the sign until it was too late! And I was in the wrong goddamn lane! Okay?"

"Turn around *now* and get back on 280 going north."

She did a tire-screeching U-turn and peeled up the entrance ramp to the highway.

"Tell me what's going on," she demanded, squeezing the steering wheel as if her hands were wrapped around his neck.

Marcel didn't respond.

"I'm almost out of gas."

He remained silent for a couple of minutes before speaking. "Get off at Page Mill Road."

"Thank you!"

"Then turn right."

With the white arrow hovering a millimeter above the letter E on her fuel gauge, she took the exit, turned onto Page Mill Road, and saw a Chevron station ahead.

"I need to stop and—"

"No. When you reach El Camino, take another right. You'll see a McDonald's. That's where you're going."

"Fuck," she uttered, now realizing that Marcel had outfoxed her.

"I repeat. When you reach—"

"I heard you the first time," Sarah snapped. Several blocks later, she saw the street sign for El Camino, made a right turn, and pulled into the McDonald's parking lot.

"Now what?"

"Go to the women's toilet and drop the sample into the trash receptacle. Then drive back to MEREIN. I'll ring you shortly."

Sarah clipped the phone to a pants pocket, turned off the engine, and got out of her car. She looked around for any suspicious-looking characters, and then walked to the restaurant and stepped inside. Several people were sitting at tables and booths. As far as she could tell, not one of them had a Neiman Marcus shopping bag. The women's restroom was to her right. She eased the door open and entered. A quick inspection confirmed she was alone. With no alternative plan and conceding that it would be unwise to disobey his order, she reached inside her handbag, removed the little white bag containing her T-3 sample, and dropped it into the trashcan.

Sarah sat on a stool in Lab 110 and peered through a microscope at a tissue paper-thin slice of mouse brain. The delicate swirl of colors and shapes resembled a miniature abstract painting. Her eyes focused on a tangle of cells, but her mind was elsewhere.

They have it.

She squeezed her eyes shut and admonished herself for giving them the sample. They'd captured her queen. Now it was time to figure out her next move. After several seconds, it came to her.

Marcel said he was going to call me.

Sarah left the lab and walked back to her office. She opened the top drawer of her desk and retrieved a Palm Organizer. Although the device had been superseded by new technology, it had a nice recording feature that she used periodically for lectures. She checked the battery level and slipped it into her handbag.

On the way out of her office, Sarah glanced at her computer monitor and did a double take. The MEREIN TEST icon was no longer on the desktop. Incredulous, she sat down, did a group search for every Word document on her computer, and arranged them by date. The one she'd just written was not there. She next arranged her documents by name but saw nothing titled "MEREIN TEST." Her jaw dropped. The T-3 report had vanished from her computer.

chapter eight

Sarah grew increasingly restless as the day dragged on, and left work at 4:17 p.m. While driving home she realized that, with all her anxiety, she'd forgotten to eat lunch. Acknowledging her growing hunger pangs, she drove downtown, found a parking spot on Broadway Avenue, and walked into *Bronze Buddha*.

After ordering takeout, she took a seat, closed her eyes, and nervously tapped her right heel. Six hours had now passed since she entered the McDonald's restroom and dropped off the sample. Yet, despite his promise, Marcel hadn't called. Perhaps he'd disappeared. And why not? He had her T-3—and most likely the million dollars he'd deposited into her checking account.

"Your stir-fry pork."

Sarah popped her eyes open and saw a waitress extending a white bag.

"Thanks," she said, and accepted her dinner. She left

the restaurant, walked back to her car, and had just gotten into the driver's seat when the flip phone rang.

She removed the Palm Organizer from her handbag, placed it on her lap, and answered the call.

"Hello?" She held the phone between her left cheek and shoulder, pressed the RECORD button on the Palm Organizer, and raised it to her chin.

"Hello?"

She tried a third time: "Hello?"

"Turn off the recording device."

His words sent a chill through her body. She scoured the area looking for any sign of him, and then obeyed his order.

"Okay, it's off. Did you get the sample?"

"Get out of your car and proceed to the sidewalk. Take the recorder with you."

She followed his instructions. After stepping up onto the sidewalk, she returned the flip phone to her cheek.

"I left the sample. Did you get it?"

"Put the device into that green trash receptacle on your right."

"It's turned off. I'm not—"

"Do as I tell you."

She reluctantly discarded her Palm Organizer.

"Why were you attempting to record my call?"

"I don't know."

"That's not a good answer. What were you planning to do with the recording?"

Sarah realized she hadn't thought that far ahead and had no idea what she was going to do with it. But she knew Marcel wouldn't believe her, so she tried to come up with an appropriate response.

"I guess . . . I was just trying to protect myself."

"Then you failed. Have you ever gone hunting?"

"No."

"I went on my first hunting trip at the age of ten. I felt a rush of excitement as my father and I ventured into the woods. But we walked for nine hours without seeing a single deer. By late afternoon we'd given up and were returning to our village. Suddenly, my father stopped and pointed ahead at a young buck drinking from a stream. To my surprise, he handed me his rifle. This was to be my initiation. I felt so proud as I raised his Mauser and took aim at the unsuspecting deer. I had a clear shot and couldn't miss because he was just standing there. But then I wondered: Should I let him finish drinking before I squeeze the trigger? Should I permit him one last look around the beautiful forest? I began to feel sorry for him and contemplated misfiring, so he could run away. Of course, I would then suffer the wrath of my father. This all weighed heavily on me at the time.

"Anyway, I suppose I'm reminded of that experience because right now I face a similar dilemma. I have the crosshairs of my riflescope fixed on you."

Sarah was hit by a shockwave, and her legs buckled. She fell against the trash can and slid awkwardly to the sidewalk. She jerked the phone to her head and took a huge breath. "Marcel! I—"

"Let me give you a piece of advice: If you're trying

to hide from a sniper, you must first know his position."

"Ma'am, are you alright?"

Sarah looked up and saw a man with a concerned expression. She nodded, but the anguish on her face belied the gesture.

"You don't believe me," Marcel said. "Maybe I'll just shoot the Good Samaritan. That might convince you."

"No!"

The man crouched in front of her. "Would you like some help?"

"Leave me alone! Get out of here!"

He stood up and walked away, cursing her. Sarah noticed a few pedestrians gawking at her from a safe distance.

"Why do you insist on being so obstinate?"

"I gave you the sample. And I haven't told anyone—I swear!"

"This all should have been so easy. But you had to challenge me. Did I not warn you of the consequences?"

"No, no. Please—"

"Tell me, Sarah: Do you still think you're so clever? Would you like to take one last look around the beautiful forest before I kill you?"

She was too paralyzed to respond. Instead, she curled up and attempted to protect her head with her right hand. Her body shook, and she started to cry.

"I put my rifle down. I'm not going to shoot you."

She didn't budge.

"Would you please get up. You're making a spectacle of yourself."

Shaking knees made it difficult to stand. She finally got to her feet, and the onlookers began to disperse.

"Go home and pull yourself together. I will ring you later."

———

Sarah was sitting at the dining room table when the flip phone rang.

Go to hell.

She reached for her Marlboro Light, took a drag, and exhaled a plume of smoke that lingered in the air. By the time she rested her cigarette on the ashtray, the phone had rung four more times. She picked up her glass of Chardonnay and took a sip, savoring it for several seconds before swallowing. The phone went silent.

Her takeout was still in the paper bag. Despite eating next to nothing all day, she had no appetite for food. But she was on her fourth glass of wine.

The phone rang again. The very idea of hearing his voice made her nauseous. But she knew he was hell-bent on talking to her, so she answered the call.

"Yes, we received your report and your T-3 sample. Thank you. I understand your drug works quite well."

She could only imagine how they made that determination. "Then I'm done," she said wearily.

"Almost. But first, they want an ingestible version of your drug."

Her stomach clenched. "An ingestible version."

"Yes. One that can be taken orally and deliver the same effect."

"It's not possible."

"Why not?"

Sarah closed her eyes and massaged her forehead. "Because it can't be done."

"Well, I'm sure you'll come up with something."

"You're crazy," she said matter-of-factly.

"And if you look, you'll see a second deposit in your checking account."

"Get rid of it."

"A total of two million dollars."

"Get it the hell out of my account!"

"Sarah, please. A little gratitude would be in order. But that's okay. You can thank me later. In the meantime, I suggest you calm down and get some sleep. You still have work ahead of you. Goodnight."

Sarah pressed the OFF button, put down the phone, and swallowed the last of her wine. She was drunk. Fatigued. Done with this. She was not going to give them anything else. And so, without much thought, she vowed to put a stop to the madness. Tomorrow.

chapter nine

———

Nursing a hangover, Sarah sat at her office desk and penned a note:

Margaret,

I was forced to give a drug sample to some dangerous people. Call the nearest FBI office using a resident's phone (DON'T use your phone or a MEREIN landline) and tell them to send someone over here immediately. The agent should pose as a journalist who has come for a pre-arranged meeting with me. We can talk openly about Alzheimer's disease, but I'm being wired, so all communication regarding the drug and my situation must be done through written notes.

Sarah stopped writing, read the directive several

times, and ripped it to shreds. Margaret would take it as a joke and say something incriminating. She could not jeopardize her friend's life—nor her own—on such a gamble.

She'd just begun to brainstorm for a new plan when the disturbing chime of the flip phone interrupted her thoughts.

"Good morning, Sarah. How are you?"

"How do you think I am?"

"Are you alone?"

"Why?"

"Because I must speak with you in private."

Sarah considered lying but decided against it. He'd talk to her at some point, so she might as well get it over with. "No one's around."

"Good. Do you remember what I told you last night?"

"No."

"Your T-3 destroys almost all brain functions when injected into the bloodstream but has no effect if taken orally."

Marcel kept speaking, but she was too stunned to absorb any more words. Her drug would horrify anyone with a conscience. But he sounded pleased and had obviously tested T-3 on something much higher up on the evolutionary ladder than a lab mouse. She imagined him approaching a homeless woman and offering her a hot meal in exchange for her participation in a new drug study.

"Sarah?"

"What?"

"I'm awaiting an answer."

"I didn't hear the question."

"Then I'll repeat. We believe stomach acid is destroying your drug after it's swallowed. Would you agree?"

"I don't know."

"But do you think it's possible?"

She hesitated. "Yeah. I guess. Stomach acid destroys a lot of things."

"I need you to access the website for Nanotechnology Labs."

"Why?" Sarah heard laughter in the hallway and got up to close her office door.

"Just do it, and I'll explain."

She returned to her computer and brought up the website.

"As you may know, Nanotechnology Labs produces polymers that microencapsulate drugs. If you scroll down, you'll see a list of their products. We're interested in the PCL and PFN. I need you to ring them and order trial samples of both. Request next-day delivery."

"You can't be serious."

"After receiving the polymers, you'll microencapsulate two ten-milliliter samples of your drug—one with PCL and the other with PFN. I'll then give you a location to drop them off. Once you've completed that task, you're finished. Now I suggest you ring Nanotechnology Labs and place the order. I'll be monitoring the call for 'quality assurance.' Goodbye."

Sarah turned off the phone and stared bug-eyed at the wall. Marcel was clearly on a mission to weaponize

T-3 and target humans. But that wasn't the only thing that unnerved her. He said she'd be "finished" after the next drop. What exactly did he mean by that? Would she be free to resume her life? After careful consideration, she decided the answer was no.

They're going to kill me.

———

Sarah's call to Nanotechnology Labs went well. The receptionist connected her to a sales representative who was more than happy to provide free samples. The products would be shipped from Europe and arrive Thursday. Marcel would have his ingestible T-3 by the end of the week. And she'd be marked for death. The small army watching her around the clock would fulfill one last task before heading to the airport. "Thank you very much, Sarah. Now close your eyes and say goodnight."

They're going to kill me.

She was surprised at how matter-of-factly she could contemplate her impending murder. It was as if the torment she'd endured since her beach encounter had drained her of any emotion. Would she be the victim of a hit-and-run? An armed robbery? A drowning? Regardless, her demise would shock friends and coworkers and perhaps warrant a small article in the *San Francisco Chronicle*—the story of a promising life erased too soon.

Sarah left her office and stepped outside. She lit a cigarette, took a puff, and exhaled skyward. "Marcel, call me."

The flip phone rang and, for the first time, she initiated the discussion. "I'm sure you heard that the polymers you want are manufactured in Switzerland. It's already Tuesday night there. I won't receive them until Thursday."

"That's not a problem. You did the best you could. Thank you."

She took another puff off her cigarette, snuffed it out, and walked back inside Building One. She entered the reference library, sat down at a computer, and did a search for "FBI offices in the Bay Area." A short list populated the screen. She read each address and concluded the nearest one was in downtown San Jose. According to Google Maps, it was a twenty-six-minute drive.

Do it.

She next did a search for "best restaurants in downtown San Jose." Marcel would surely call and question why she left MEREIN. "I'm taking a long lunch," she'd tell him. He might smell a rat and order her to turn around. But at this point, there was no going back. She'd slam the accelerator and fly like a bat out of hell. Blow past every car. Run red lights. If necessary, drive on the sidewalk like they do in action movies. Upon reaching the FBI building, she'd screech to a halt, abandon her car, and dash inside.

Marcel would know she double-crossed him. So what? Before he had time to react, she'd call Paul and tell him his life was in danger. He could hide in a safe, secure location at his workplace and wait until the Feds arrived. As soon as he was in protective custody, she'd explain her plight and ask him one question: "Who did you tell?" Had he filed an ethics charge against her? Had he told a coworker about her experiment? The objective would be to get names, phone numbers, email addresses, and other pertinent information. The FBI would then spring into action, follow the leads to Marcel, and take him down before he knew what hit him. Boom. Done deal.

Marcel called shortly after she got onto Highway 280. She unclipped the phone from a pants pocket and flipped it open. "Yeah?"

"Where are you going?"

"San Jose."

"Why?"

"To eat lunch."

"That doesn't make sense."

"My favorite restaurant is downtown. I drive there once a week for lunch and order enough takeout to last two nights. It's my routine."

"I see. Okay, then. Enjoy your lunch," he said and ended the call.

Sarah drove the remaining twenty miles without further interruption and pulled into a convenient parking spot. She fed the meter, walked to the intersection, and looked up. There it was. Right across the street. The high-rise building with an FBI office on the tenth floor. Just fifty steps away.

She blended into a group of people waiting for the light to change. Her heartbeat and respiration increased with each passing second and, although it was a cold, gray day, she felt overheated in her windbreaker. A drop of sweat tickled as it traveled down her right underarm.

The light turned green, and she proceeded across the street, doing her best to stay in the middle of the group. Whether true or not, being surrounded by others somehow gave her a sense of protection.

Sarah had almost reached the building when she noticed a young woman standing next to the entrance. She was wearing black sunglasses, which seemed odd considering the overcast sky. And she was holding a gold Neiman Marcus shopping bag identical to the one Marcel had at the beach. Sarah froze when she realized the woman was staring at her.

What are you doing? You can't just stand here!

With her mind spinning, she got down on one knee and fiddled with her left shoelace.

You're ten feet from the door. Do it!

She stole a glance at the woman. Black jacket. Tan pants. Blond hair. Ominous sunglasses. Motionless.

She retied the lace and stood. The woman was still staring at her. Neither of them moved. Then the woman stuck her right hand inside the shopping bag.

Sarah gasped and reluctantly aborted her plan. Struggling to place one foot in front of the other, she walked past the mystery woman and sensed a pair of eyes piercing her back. She took deep breaths and tried to grapple with the fact that they'd been waiting for her. They knew her plan. But how? The answer came like a gut punch.

"*Shit.* They're monitoring the goddamn computer," she whispered to herself.

The flip phone rang, and she stopped to answer it.

"You're lucky to be alive," Marcel said, his voice frighteningly calm. "Had you tried to enter that building, I'm quite sure we wouldn't be having this conversation. But let's assume you made it inside. Going to the FBI would make my employer very angry. In retaliation, I guarantee you he'd microencapsulate T-3 without your assistance and carry out attacks against civilians. And he'd send an interesting story to the media—the story of a woman who secretly created a brain-destroying drug and sold it to terrorists for two million dollars. Of course, you'd claim you meant no harm when you conducted your experiment and insist you were forced to provide a sample. But your appeals for forgiveness would be met with scorn. And your name would forever be associated with acts of domestic terrorism.

"Think about it.

"Oh, and by the way, you're right. We *are* monitoring that computer. Goodbye."

———

Standing outside of Building One and smoking another Marlboro Light, Sarah scolded herself for failing to think through her escape plan. Marcel was right. So what if she reached the FBI? Sure, she could impress them with the flip phone and the anklet. Show them the million-dollar bank deposits. Give a description of him. But the FBI, Homeland Security, or anyone else brought in would have little to work with.

And going to the FBI would bring fire to their eyes. Assuming they microencapsulated T-3 without her assistance—and it's likely they could—they'd make sure she paid for her defiance.

She imagined them injecting T-3 into cartons of milk

being delivered to an elementary school. At lunchtime on a sunny day in the heartland of America, children would collapse and become unresponsive. The news would go viral and shock the civilized world. In newspaper articles and on television screens, her photo would appear alongside those of cherubic kids whose lives had been destroyed. It was a possibility she could not risk.

Running to the Feds was out of the question. But, on the other hand, she couldn't provide them samples and hope they'd disappear from her life. Her adversaries had invested too much time, money, and resources to acquire T-3 and plan an attack. They would not assume she'd keep quiet—even with a princely sum of money in her checking account. They'd make sure she couldn't ruin their surprise.

Sarah returned to her office, locked the door, and curled up in a ball on the floor. She pressed her forehead to her knees and tried to come up with something. Anything. But her mind drew a blank. There seemed to be no way out of her predicament.

Mentally slipping into a dark space, she contemplated suicide. She'd call Rogelio, confess her sin, and tell him how much she loved him. After saying goodbye, she'd inject herself with a combination of drugs that would ensure a painless death.

But as she considered which drugs to take—most of them arranged alphabetically inside the refrigerator in Lab 110—she snapped out of her depression and cursed herself for wallowing in self-pity. She didn't want to die. And killing herself would guarantee the bastards won. With no one to stop them, Marcel and his gang would produce an ingestible T-3 and use it for god-knows-what. There was no way in hell she could allow that to happen. Not without a fight. She refocused her brain, and within a couple of minutes came up with an ingenious idea: a two-step escape plan.

Step One: Remove the anklet and withdraw the two million dollars. Leave a note next to the discarded anklet telling Marcel they were even—he had her T-3, and she had the money. He could do whatever he wanted with her drug, and she wouldn't tell anyone. Hopefully, he'd believe it.

Step Two: Buy a prepaid, untraceable phone. Call NYU and convince someone to hand Paul a message that read, "This is Sarah. Call me ASAP but do *not* use your personal or work phone. Borrow one from the person who just gave you this note." When Paul called, she'd explain her predicament, and together they'd come up with a plan to alert the FBI.

She went over every detail of her two-step plan and concluded it was doable. However, there was one small catch: she'd have to figure out how to remove the anklet, evade the small army, and withdraw the two million dollars before Marcel noticed.

Sarah left her office and took a familiar path to the gymnasium. This time she made it inside without getting a call from Marcel. She walked past the basketball courts and yoga studio and entered the women's locker room.

Almost every employee and resident at MEREIN had a locker. Each was unique. Some were elaborately painted or decorated with photos. Others simply had a name printed on the front. Hers was the only one with a picture of a warthog.

She changed into sweatpants and a T-shirt and walked to a mirror-lined room stocked with Nautilus equipment, stationary bicycles, and free weights. She mounted a Lifecycle and began pedaling. The flip phone bobbed up and down on her right hip, and the ankle bracelet made 160 rpm circles. She hoped that, in some telepathic way, Marcel would get dizzy.

The workout provided a perfect opportunity to brainstorm, and she used every charge of the pedals to think of ways to remove the anklet and withdraw the two million dollars. Twenty minutes later, exhausted, and with a drop of sweat dangling from her chin, the imaginary light bulb illuminated above her head. She stopped pedaling and let the machine's internal generator slow to a halt.

Sarah returned to the locker room, showered, and got dressed. While walking back to her office, she acknowledged the risks in her escape plan and thought of something that might improve her odds. She could effuse a more pragmatic Sarah who, realizing she couldn't beat them, decided to cooperate. After all, who could resist a two-million-dollar carrot? Without overdoing it, she could play the obedient woman doing her best in exchange for an early retirement. Maybe, just maybe, they'd lower their guard.

"Marcel, call me."

She heard the discordant ringtone and opened the phone. "I thought about what you said. You're right. Going to the FBI would be a stupid idea. So, I'll make your next round of samples. And you have my word. I won't tell anyone."

"Good. That's what I wanted to hear."

"I also want to keep the two million dollars."

There was a pause in the conversation before Marcel continued. "I'm curious. Why did you change your mind?"

"Let's be honest with each other. I know you're trying to bribe me. But I don't care. After what I've been through, I think I've earned it. And frankly, I could use the money. Does that answer your question?"

"Yes. I appreciate your candor," he said. "The two million dollars will remain in your account. But be careful. Years ago, a federal employee was supplying us classified information. In exchange, he was generously rewarded. Unfortunately, he became obsessed with the dichotomy between his modest existence and available fortune. So, one day he purchased a Jaguar. The automobile. Then he bought a home in Rockville, Maryland, where no one making his salary could afford to live. That surprised his coworkers. I'll spare you the details of the investigation. Suffice to say, he's still in prison. So, I raise this as a cautionary tale. The money is quite seductive."

"I understand."

"The two million dollars will remain in your account. In exchange, you'll provide the microencapsulated samples. Do you agree?"

"Yes."

"Good," Marcel said. "I think it's best we work together."

chapter ten

Sitting on her living room couch, Sarah thought long and hard before gaining the courage to proceed with Step One of her escape plan. First order of business: remove the ankle transmitter. Its two semi-circular components were held together by a hinge and a latching mechanism. The hinge pin was the weak link. If she could construct a tool to remove it, she might be able to pry the two sections apart just enough to slip her foot through.

Dusk was succumbing to night as Sarah left the house and walked to the storage shed in her backyard. She unlocked the door, went inside, and flipped the light switch. In front of her was a workbench constructed entirely of two-by-fours. Above the workbench, a sheet of plywood was mounted to the wall, and held an assortment of her landlord's hand tools.

Sarah perused the tools and selected a three-inch C-clamp. She then looked inside a plastic bin filled with miscellaneous hardware and pulled out a flathead, 6-32 machine screw. Its diameter appeared to be a bit smaller than the hinge pin on her anklet. She opened drawers of a hardware cabinet and found one filled with washers. She picked one and, after verifying the machine screw could fit through it, selected seven more washers of the same size.

On the wall to her right were shelves stocked with paint, lubricants, and various adhesives. She saw a tube of Metal Bond and unscrewed the cap to make sure it was still usable.

Sarah returned to the house with her supplies and locked the back door. Her iPhone rang. She saw that the call was from Rogelio and decided not to answer it. The phone stopped ringing, and she received a text message: "Where RU?"

Before she could decide how to respond, the flip phone rang.

"What?"

"Rogelio is driving back from Southern California, and I see he's trying to get in touch with you," Marcel said.

"I know."

"Again, if you wish your boyfriend no harm, you'll avoid any contact with him for a few days."

"And what am I supposed to do if he just shows up at my house?"

"Get rid of him."

"How?"

"You're an intelligent woman. You'll think of something. Goodbye."

"Fuck you," Sarah said and slammed the phone shut. She threw it on the kitchen table, pulled out her iPhone, and composed a text message to Rogelio: "Hi sweetie. I've been working on that article for three hours. I'm exhausted. Going to bed in ten minutes. See you in a few days. Love you!" She read the message twice and sent it.

Sarah walked into the living room, heard the unmistakable chime, and ran back to the kitchen. She grabbed the flip phone off the table and answered his call.

"Marcel, I—"

"This is the second or third time you've broken the two-meter rule."

"I'm sorry! I'm trying my best, okay?"

"Don't do it again."

Sarah suppressed an urge to punch the wall. Instead, she took several deep breaths and clipped the phone to her belt. She returned to the living room, pulled the French-language erotic thriller *Le Nuit de l'inconnu* from her DVD collection, and inserted it into the player. She turned on the television and started the movie, hoping its steamy dialogue might distract her nemesis.

Sarah placed her supplies on the couch and sat down. She removed the cap from the tube of Metal Bond, dabbed a thin layer of the gray paste onto the face of one washer, and pressed another washer to it. She then deposited adhesive to the outer face of the second washer and secured a third one. She continued this process until she'd constructed a cylindrical stack of eight washers. Next, she applied some Metal Bond to the head of the machine screw and glued it to the

C-clamp's fixed jaw. To the adjustable jaw, she glued the stack of washers.

After the Metal Bond became tacky, she turned the C-clamp handle until the machine screw and washers almost touched. She then re-positioned the screw so that it was centered above the hole in the stack of washers. Just like that, she'd made a custom-made hinge-pin remover.

The tiny instructions on the tube of Metal Bond recommended thirty minutes for drying. It seemed a good time to pause the movie and eat dinner. Except for one thing: she wasn't hungry. She drank a glass of wine and smoked a cigarette, hoping the combination of alcohol and nicotine would calm her nerves and induce an appetite. It didn't work. Nothing in the refrigerator appealed to her palate—not the salmon, the green beans, or even the container of yogurt. She closed the refrigerator, opened a kitchen cabinet, and pulled out a box of wheat crackers and a jar of peanut butter.

———

Sarah returned to the living room after eating four peanut butter and cracker sandwiches and sat on the couch. She resumed *Le Nuit de l'inconnu* and examined her new hinge-pin remover. The Metal Bond had hardened. The little tool was ready for use.

Suddenly, unexpected noises came from just outside the front door. Sarah muted the movie and heard someone trying to turn the doorknob. She frantically grabbed her supplies and tossed them under the couch. As she turned off the TV, she recognized the clicking sound of the front door unlocking. Rogelio opened the door and stepped inside. Sarah jumped to her feet and faced him. "Wow. What a surprise."

"I thought you were going to bed."

"I was but—"

"I'm glad you didn't." He walked over to her, and they shared a hug and a passionate kiss. "I missed you so much."

"I missed you too, sweetie."

"Whoa," he said, stepping back. "You smell like cigarette smoke."

She offered a guilty smile. "Oops, I guess I'm busted."

"You're smoking again."

"Not really. I just bought one pack for this week."

"Why?"

"Because of that article I'm writing."

Rogelio squeezed her shoulders. "Sarah, that's not good. You'd stopped smoking. You were doing so well."

"I know, but this article is stressing me out."

He gave her a mischievous look. "Hey, I know a better way to relieve stress. Let me give you a massage."

Her heart thumped. "No, no. I'm okay. Really."

"Come on, let's use up the last of that massage oil."

"I'd love to, but you know what happens. It starts as a massage, and then, before you know it, we're—"

"And what's wrong with that?" He smiled and kissed her forehead.

"Nothing. It's just that I don't have time right now."

"A ten-minute massage. That's it. I promise." Rogelio took her hand and began pulling her toward the bedroom.

"No."

"Come on. It'll do you good."

"Stop it," Sarah insisted, ripping her hand free from his grasp.

His smile became a scowl. "Hey! What's the matter with you?"

"I just told you. I don't have time to play around."

"You don't have ten minutes? Are you shittin' me? We haven't seen each other in a week. I drove thirty miles out of my way to see you, and you won't even give me *ten minutes*?"

She had no answer and stared at the floor.

"What's going on?"

"Nothing. I'm just worried about making my deadline."

He squeezed his lips together. "Show me what you've written."

"No."

"Why not?"

"I'll show it to you when it's done, okay?" She forced a smile. "We'll celebrate."

He narrowed his eyes on her. "You got another guy over here?"

"No. How could you say that?"

"Because you're acting strange. And you don't look very happy to see me."

She inhaled and exhaled a deep breath. "Look, I need to get back to work. Maybe you should leave."

Rogelio's cold stare suggested he wanted to strangle her. Instead, he turned and walked to the front door.

"Sweetie, I'm sorry," she called out. "This is just a bad week for me."

He spun around. "No, you're wrong. It's a bad week for *us*." With that, he stormed out of the house and slammed the door shut behind him.

Sarah dropped her head and cursed. Fighting back tears, she locked the front door, went to the kitchen, and poured herself another glass of Chardonnay. She took a sip and heard the chime. With trembling hands, she unclipped the flip phone and raised it to her left cheek.

"Very good, Sarah," Marcel said. "You handled that well."

——

The second glass of wine did little to ease her anxiety over the fight with Rogelio. It did, however, boost her determination to continue with the escape plan.

Sarah returned to the living room, resumed *Le Nuit de l'inconnu*, and retrieved the hinge-pin remover from under the couch. She crossed her left foot over her right knee and pulled up the leg of her sweatpants to reveal the anklet. She positioned her new tool and turned the C-clamp handle until the machine screw and stack of washers came into contact with the anklet. She aligned the machine screw with the hinge pin and gave the handle two turns. The pin put up resistance but was no match for her new tool. She gave it another turn and stopped. There was no call from Marcel. Another half turn. Still no call. The next turn offered no resistance. She spun the handle counterclockwise and removed the tool. The shiny hinge pin fell onto the rug, and there was now a hole in the anklet.

Sarah carefully pried apart the two semi-circular halves, revealing an eighth-inch-wide metallic ribbon. She guessed the ribbon was part of an alarm circuit that became activated when Marcel clamped the transmitter around her ankle. Unlatching the anklet or otherwise interrupting the electrical current path through it would trigger an alarm. She continued prying apart the two anklet halves until the ribbon became taut. Despite increasing the anklet's diameter, she still couldn't slide it past her heel and feared putting additional pressure on the ribbon might cause it to break.

She made a trip to the storage shed and found a soldering iron, a roll of solder, an X-Acto knife, a piece of insulated wire, and an extension cord.

Back in the living room, she plugged one end of the extension cord into a wall socket and the other to the soldering iron. By the time she sat down on the couch and got comfortable, the silver tip of the iron was emitting a fine column of gray smoke. With her left foot propped up on her right knee, she soldered both ends of the two-inch wire to the exposed section of gold ribbon. The molten solder cooled, and the connections seemed strong enough to withstand a fair amount of tension.

Grasping the X-Acto knife in her right hand, she poked a tiny hole in the ribbon between the two solder joints and made delicate sawing motions. The ribbon snapped apart, and a jolt of terror rocked her body. An agonizing minute passed with her eyes glued to the flip phone. Two minutes passed. Three minutes and still no call from Marcel. She was now confident her theory was right. Even though she'd severed the ribbon, her newly soldered wire served as an alternate path for the electrical current.

She gripped the two anklet halves and again began prying them apart. This time it wasn't the ribbon but the latch that put up resistance. To her dismay, she still couldn't remove the loathsome device.

It was one of those moments in life when anger overcomes good judgment. She picked up the soldering iron and stuck its 800-degree tip into the hinge-pin hole in one of the anklet halves. Inhaling acrid fumes, she watched as the iron burned away a piece of material.

Sarah set the soldering iron down and was able to slide the anklet past her heel. She hadn't expected success and gushed a silent scream of jubilation. She looked at what was now a disfigured heap of plastic and a loop of wire and worried the mutilation might have impugned its electrical integrity.

She unclipped the flip phone from her waistband, placed it on the couch next to the discarded anklet, and walked to the far end of the room. She stood still for five minutes. Marcel didn't call.

Now emboldened to continue with her escape plan, she pulled the extension cord from the wall socket and cut off both ends. She walked to her studio, unplugged the microphone from the music workstation, cut its cord in half, and spliced the extension cord between the two lengths. Her microphone now had a thirty-foot reach.

Sarah plugged the cord back into the workstation and launched *Music Maker* software. An array of menus and musical symbols filled her computer screen. She clicked NEW SONG, named it "Cough," and hit TRACK 1 > RECORD. She carried the microphone into her bedroom and set it on the nightstand. She coughed, went back to the studio, and hit STOP. The screen displayed a waveform of the nineteen-second recording. It was almost entirely a flat line, except for a noticeable spike midway through. She hit PLAY. A cursor started from the beginning of the recording and moved left to right along the sound pattern as numerals counted the elapsed seconds. She heard nothing until the curser passed the ten-second mark. At that moment, a distinct cough played through her speakers. One cough. It was enough to confirm that her newly spliced microphone was functioning.

Sarah returned to the bedroom, pulled a pair of long underwear from a dresser, and cut two inches of elastic material from the bottom of one leg. Back at the couch, she slid the anklet over her left foot, and secured it with the ring of elastic. To test its reliability, she shook her leg and jumped up and down several times. The two-inch piece of elastic held the anklet in place.

With newfound confidence in her escape plan, she paused *Le Nuit de l'inconnu*, turned off the TV, and prepared for bed. Just before getting under the covers, she went to the studio and started a new recording titled "Sleep."

chapter eleven

————

Sarah silenced the clock radio alarm. Its red numerals displayed 7:00 a.m. She peeled the blanket and sheet away from her body and pivoted her feet to the floor. Fawn-like steps took her out of the bedroom and into the studio. She brought up the *Music Maker* screen and looked at her new "Sleep" recording. Not surprising, there was little seismic activity on the waveform. And the software's two-hour-per-song limit meant the recording had stopped shortly after midnight.

She started another recording titled "Neil" and crept back to the bedroom. She stroked the mattress with her hands and rustled covers to replicate getting out of bed. A flip of the light switch bathed the room in a soft glow. She called Neil's office phone, held the microphone next to her cheek to record his voicemail greeting, and then left him a message: "Hi, this is Sarah. I'm afraid I might be coming down with a cold. I'm gonna try to get some more sleep. I'll probably be in later." With that, she carried the microphone to the studio, stopped the "Neil" recording, and got back into bed.

Staring at the ceiling, she again dissected her escape plan. Would her recordings fool Marcel and his crew? Just how high-tech were they? Given her top-of-the-line equipment, she knew the sound quality would be excellent. But could she fool them?

Assuming the best, how would it feel to escape? Assuming the worst, how would it feel to be killed? She'd read that fatal gunshots aren't so excruciating because shock kicks in and suppresses the pain you'd expect to feel after getting your guts blasted open. You fall down and go to sleep. Was that true or just wishful thinking?

She tossed in bed—coughing periodically to help sell her impending cold—and watched minutes tick by on her clock. After what seemed an eternity, 8:00 a.m. came and went. Then 8:30. And finally, 9:00. It was time to get dressed and drive to work.

Sarah unlocked the top drawer of her desk, removed the vial of T-3, and dropped it inside her handbag. She left her office, headed down the hallway, and entered Lab 110. Two interns studying brain images on a computer monitor looked up and smiled at her before returning to their work. She walked over to a refrigerator, opened it, surveyed the multitude of drugs, and found a vial of the powerful sedative Entoryl-XT.

While walking back to her office, she ran into Neil. "I got your message. How are you feeling?" he asked.

"Like I might be coming down with a cold."

"Then I'd prefer you stay home. I believe you infected half the department last year."

She offered a contrite smile. "I promise to stay in my office. And I'll go home early."

"Go home now. I insist."

———

Sarah had no appetite but knew her body needed complex carbohydrates, protein, and a little fat to provide needed energy for her escape. She prepared a dinner of salmon, brown rice, and steamed broccoli and forced herself to eat it. A large glass of Pinot Grigio helped ease her unsettled stomach.

After dinner, she started the dishwasher, wiped off the counters, and dried her hands with a terry cloth towel. She sat down at the kitchen table, lit a cigarette, and penned an appeal:

> *Dear Marcel,*
>
> *By the time you read this note, I've escaped and taken the two million dollars. I had no choice. We both know you were going to kill me.*
>
> *Now we're even—you have my T-3 and I have your money. Leave me alone and I won't go to the authorities.*
>
> *Sincerely,*
> *Sarah*

She tucked the note into an envelope and wrote "Marcel" on the outside.

Next, she wrote a letter to Rogelio, explaining that she was leaving him to start a new life far away from California. She knew Marcel would read it first. It was sucker bait to protect her boyfriend and help convince the hit squad she'd left town and wasn't a threat.

She took a puff off her Marlboro Light and realized that if all went according to plan, Marcel might be in custody within twenty-four hours.

But what if things went south? The woman with the black sunglasses and the gun in her shopping bag could show up again and prevent her from going to the FBI. Or she might wind up running for her life and hiding out for a day. Or a few days. She remembered her Girl Scout motto—"Be Prepared"—and decided to pack some clothes and withdraw a fair amount of cash from the bank. Just in case.

She extinguished her cigarette, walked into the bedroom, and found her backpack hanging in the closet. Without making a sound, she filled it with enough clothes to last a week and added a toiletry bag and a pocketknife.

While wondering what else to take, it occurred to her that Marcel might torch her house. Although it seemed unlikely, she packed her mother and father's wedding rings, her birth certificate, and passport.

She went into her studio, opened a desk drawer, and removed two flash drives. One was labeled "Music." It contained dozens of her own compositions, along with songs from various recording artists. The second drive, labeled "Photos," held more than 8,000 images. Feeling a bit sentimental and realizing that Marcel could be moving in for the kill, she decided to take some time and do a fitting celebration of her life.

She plugged the flash drive into her iMac and filled the screen with photos. She scrolled to the top and started with the digitized 35-millimeter snapshots from her early years: blowing out six candles on her birthday cake, playing *Edelweiss* at a piano recital, showing off her gold medal after winning a 400-meter race, selling Girl Scout cookies, posing in her karate uniform.

Further down, some family photographs: a trip to Disneyland, fishing with her parents at Clear Lake, a picnic at Ocean Beach, camping in a state park, building a robot in the garage with her father.

She scrolled to some photos of her at age fifteen: black jeans, Doc Marten boots, spiky hair. Looking tough. It was a tough period indeed. Shattered by her father's death, she'd turned to drugs and was living the wild life until her best friend died of an overdose. That prompted a visit to the high school student counselor, who steered her away from higher times and toward higher grades.

Then a photo out of chronological order: her mother, Cathleen, just twenty-one years old, sitting on a blanket in Golden Gate Park. She studied the image and was again struck by the beauty of her mother's cheekbones and Rapunzel-like hair.

The next group of photographs documented her high school years, culminating with one of her in a royal blue gown at the graduation ceremony. Her proud mother was standing at her side, holding a letter announcing a partial scholarship to Stanford University.

She fast-forwarded twelve years to a poignant photograph. In it, she was hugging Cathleen on her fifty-seventh birthday. By then, her mother's body had surrendered to ovarian cancer, and she was old beyond her years. The disease had spared her cheekbones but little else. Her flowing hair had been reduced to mere wisps, covered with a headscarf. Her green eyes no longer sparkled and the smile of the free spirit sitting on a blanket in Golden Gate Park was now bittersweet.

Sarah continued her celebration of life and eventually got to the last photograph: she and Rogelio at Ristorante Primavera. Arm in arm. Radiant smiles. Dressed to the nines. It was taken by a waiter the evening they celebrated the anniversary of their first date.

She gazed longingly at the photo, bit her lip, and made a vow not to die any time soon. She'd beat the bastards and add many more photographs to her life story. And she'd start with another one of her and Rogelio at Ristorante Primavera—this time celebrating their engagement.

Infused with a new sense of purpose, she pulled the flash drive from her computer, and packed it along with the "Music" drive.

She removed the two drug vials from her handbag and drew fifteen milliliters of Entoryl-XT into a syringe. After covering the tip with a safety cap, she wrapped the syringe and vials together and added them to her backpack.

She now had three lethal weapons at her disposal—a pocketknife and two drugs—and decided that Entoryl-

XT would be her first choice if Marcel confronted her again. Unlike T-3, which took a minute to kick in, the potent anesthetic would knock him out in three seconds. She could escape and call 911. Marcel would wake up in the back seat of a police car.

Another major advantage of Entoryl-XT was that it wouldn't destroy his brain. Getting him to talk would be crucial to solving the T-3 mystery and hopefully averting a terrorist attack.

Sarah went to the living room, turned on the television, and channel-surfed to something truly grotesque: Five young women were chained together at their ankles. An uncontrollable blonde was screaming that she hated one of her co-chainees while being ordered, "Shut the **BEEP** up, you **BEEP** before I slap the **BEEP** out of you." Another masterpiece of family entertainment from the geniuses at Reality TV.

She sat down, slid the anklet past her left heel, and placed it on the couch next to the flip phone. She then went to the studio and gently closed the door behind her. Sitting in front of the computer screen, she donned a headset, copied from the "Neil" recording his voicemail greeting, and pasted it at 1:59.30 of the two-hour "Sleep" recording. She aligned the cursor with the end of Neil's greeting, hit RECORD, and spoke into the microphone: "Hi, this is Sarah. I'm feeling better today, but I could still use some more sleep. I should be in before ten." She hit STOP and checked the recording. It was perfect.

She went back to the living room, watched the five

chained women debate who was the most reviled of the bunch, and decided it would be a tough call. She slipped the transmitter and elastic over her ankle, clipped the flip phone to her pocket, and turned off the TV.

She laid out a set of clean clothes next to her computer, moved one of the Bose speakers to her nightstand, unbraided her hair, and took a shower.

Before going to bed, she found the partially filled pack of Marlboro Lights and—without remorse or fanfare—dropped it into a wastebasket.

chapter twelve

Sarah returned from the bathroom at 5:17 a.m., sat on the edge of her bed, and put the flip phone back on her nightstand. The glass of water she'd consumed six hours earlier as a wake-up alarm had proved unnecessary as anxiety kept her vigilant most of the night. Her eyes had stared endlessly into darkness, and she enjoyed only a few episodes of sleep before snapping awake and checking the time.

For the past hour, she'd mentally reviewed her plan of action with the meticulousness of a general before combat. Over and over, she scrutinized each step of her impending escape. And now, sitting upright and rocking nervously, she watched the clock radio numerals advance to 5:19 a.m. This was it; no more what-ifs or debate. Fatigue and adrenaline combined. She had no energy but could run a marathon. A strange sensation. Enough of this madness; it was time to go.

She removed the anklet, placed it on her night-stand next to the flip phone, and walked to the studio. One jiggle of the mouse caused the monitor to explode in bright colors. After her dilated pupils recovered, she highlighted her recorded sleep track, selected the REPEAT function so that the two-hour segment would run continuously, and clicked PLAY.

She braided her hair and dressed by the light of the computer screen. Black jeans. Green turtleneck. Black hoodie. Running shoes. Her fingers quivered while tying the laces. She strapped on her backpack, left the studio, and paused at the bedroom. The Bose speaker perched on her nightstand emanated a faint rustling noise.

She tiptoed to the pantry, grabbed a small ladder, and eased open the back door. Her heart pounded like a kick drum as she stepped outside into a spitting rain. She walked across moist grass to the redwood fence and planted the A-frame ladder on the ground. After making sure it was stable, she climbed three steps and sat on top of the fence. She raised her legs, pivoted her body, and jumped down into her neighbor's garden. Her eyes darted from one end of the backyard to the other. To her amazement—and relief—there was no sign of Marcel or anyone else. She snuck around the side of the house and pushed open a gate. It made a creaking sound.

Suddenly, ear-piercing barks jolted the morning calm. Sarah broke into a sprint as the Rottweilers howled and attacked their chain-link barrier. She raced down Clinton Court, anticipating a human voice. Or a gunshot. Never had she been so terrified. Never had she run so fast. At Oak Street, she veered left and continued down an alley. The barking ceased, and now she heard only the mantra of her running feet and breathing. Legs propelling. Lungs pumping. Machine-like.

To her surprise, the Rottweilers erupted again. She screeched to a halt and crouched behind a trashcan. Breathing mightily, she looked back. She could hear the dogs but saw nothing. Then a car appeared. It proceeded slowly down Oak Street and came to a stop at the alley. Someone in the front passenger seat shined a powerful flashlight in her direction. Its beam scanned the area and passed just above her head. She held her breath and didn't so much as blink. After a thorough flashlight sweep of the alley, the car drove away.

Sarah sprang to her feet and regained her Olympian stride. Darkened scenery whizzed by in a blur. In two blocks, the alley ended, and she had no choice but to turn onto El Camino Real, a well-lit thoroughfare. At the first intersection, she ducked down a side street that offered better cover and raced past darkened shops, deserted buildings, and two homeless encampments. The cold raindrops battering her face infused her with vigor, and she maintained a remarkable pace. But not for long. As she entered the final stretch, her lungs and leg muscles started to burn. She craved a brief rest but knew there was no time. She willed her body on and jogged past an auto dealership and through a large shopping mall parking lot before staggering across her finish line—the Caltrain platform.

Sarah doubled over, her braids almost touching the ground. Soaked with rain and sweat and battling for oxygen, she massaged her cramping thigh muscles and wondered if she'd actually escaped. She heard the welcome air horn of a train, looked up, and saw its headlight in the distance.

"Yes!" she exclaimed.

The 5:40 a.m. express train to San Francisco pulled into the station—right on schedule. She boarded with a handful of others and allowed herself the luxury of a smile.

I did it. I fucking did it!

———

Antoine Boucher was two hours into his shift at the command center when he heard Sarah shuffling in bed. He increased the volume on his desk speakers and listened as she placed a phone call. He heard five rings, and then: "Hello. You've reached Neil Obergaard. Please leave a message." **BEEP**

"Hi, this is Sarah. I'm feeling better today, but I could still use some more sleep. I should be in before ten."

He opened the Sarah Logbook and typed his first entry of the day:

7:21. Sarah called work. Feeling better, but going back to bed. Will be in by 10:00.

———

A security guard unlocked the front door to the bank and allowed in four customers who'd lined up against an outside wall. Sarah viewed the action from her seat in a bus stop shelter. She stood and waited for the traffic light to turn green. It was time to collect her due.

She crossed Market Street, entered the bank, and was soon directed to a white-haired gentleman seated behind a desk. A gold nameplate with black letters identified him as Fred Colvin.

Sarah sat down in a chair facing him and did her best to remain calm. "Hi. I'd like to withdraw two million dollars from my checking account."

To her surprise, Mr. Colvin didn't bat an eye. Considering the number of billionaires who live in San Francisco, and the huge sums of money that flow in and out of this bank, it was likely her request didn't faze him.

"May I have your user ID and password?"

He entered her information into his computer and asked for her social security number, mother's maiden name, and bank card PIN. He stared at his screen for some time, and she worried the million-dollar deposits had triggered a red flag.

He turned to her. "You don't want this much money in a checking account. I would suggest putting it in a CD or another account with a higher APY."

"I'll think about that. But right now, I just want a cashier's check for two million and a thousand dollars in cash. Whatever money is left can stay in my account."

"Okay. Please know that we're required by law to report to the IRS any withdrawals of ten thousand dollars or greater."

"That's no problem."

"Very well then. A cashier's check in the amount of two million dollars, and a thousand in cash."

Sarah nodded. "Yes."

Then she reconsidered her request. Marcel was undoubtedly monitoring her Visa and ATM cards. Until this nightmare was over, she'd have to conduct all her financial transactions in cash. What if she was forced into hiding for a week? Would a thousand dollars be enough?

"I'm sorry. Make that ten thousand."

"As you wish," Mr. Colvin said. He typed a few keystrokes, printed out a document, and placed it in front of her. "I need your signature."

She signed at the bottom, and he got up from his chair. "I'll be right back."

He returned a few minutes later and handed her a cashier's check. Her eyes bulged. It was made out to Sarah Brenalen in the amount of $2,000,000. She folded the check and slid it into her wallet.

"Please follow me," he said and escorted her to a windowless office. Sarah stepped inside and saw an armed security guard standing next to a desk. Three ceiling-mounted cameras pointed at her. She cursed under her breath, fearing Mr. Colvin had brought her here for an interrogation.

"Have a seat."

She sat in a chair facing the desk, and her stomach started to churn.

"In what denominations would you like your withdrawal?"

Sarah cleared her throat. "One-hundred-dollar bills please."

He left the room, and all was quiet—with the exception of her pounding heart. She took several deep breaths and studied her fingernails. Her right heel began tapping the carpet, and she forced it to stop. The security guard stared at her but didn't say a word. Was he analyzing her body language?

Fifteen minutes. That's it. You'll be outta here in fifteen minutes.

Mr. Colvin returned with two stacks of bills and set them on the desk. He grabbed one of the stacks, removed its paper band, and placed it on the tray of a small machine. He pressed a button. She heard a whirring sound and saw red numbers counting. When the whirring stopped, the readout displayed $5,000. He reattached the paper band around the stack and set it in front of her. He took the second stack and put it on the tray. Button press. Whir. Another $5,000.

———

At 9:21 a.m. Antoine Boucher was busy at the command center computer. He'd just put the nine of hearts on the ten of spades when he heard Sarah rouse from sleep and call MEREIN a second time. "Hi, this is Sarah. I'm feeling better today, but I could still use some more sleep. I should be in before ten."

Antoine minimized the Solitaire screen, opened the Sarah Logbook, and typed a second entry. After giving it a read, he saved it and went back to the game. Within a minute, he'd lost again. Frustrated, he got up from his chair and walked toward the coffee maker to get a refill. Halfway there, he stopped. Something was bugging him besides his ineptitude at Solitaire. Something about his latest entry. Returning to his seat at the computer, he opened the Sarah Logbook, and reread it carefully.

> *9:21. Sarah called work again. Same thing. Going back to sleep. Will be in before 10:00.*

He immediately saw the problem. She'd left the message at 9:21 a.m. How could she go back to bed, get more sleep, and still make it to MEREIN in less than forty minutes?

He closed the logbook, opened the voice tracker, and scrolled back in time to her 7:21 a.m. call. He listened to it. And again. It sounded eerily similar to her latest call. He selected the Grab tool and created a dotted, rectangular box around the voice pattern. He hit COPY, changed the color from green to red, and pasted it below the voice pattern of her 9:21 call.

No, the two messages were not *similar*. They were *identical*.

Now starting to panic, he opened the Transmitter 1 screen. The map showed the anklet still inside Sarah's house. He breathed a sigh of relief. But his relief was short-lived. He remembered Transmitter 2—the Smart Pebble Marcel had attached to her running shoe at the beach. Erika had silenced the device because it was triggering false alarms. He opened the Transmitter 2 screen and experienced a jolt of incredulity. A flashing white dot showed its location. It was in downtown San Francisco.

If it was any consolation, he was not the only one in shock. Marcel had just received a long-distance phone call from his boss. The two million dollars they'd deposited into Sarah's bank account was gone.

———

Sarah walked down Market Street, periodically glancing over her shoulder.

I did it. Unbelievable. So, tell me, Marcel: Do you still think you're so clever? Huh? Would you like to take one last look around your little cubicle before they put a bullet through your skull? May the image of my face haunt you as you gasp your last breaths. Au revoir, Marcel. Au revoir.

At Beale Street she looked for the phone store and saw just ahead its signature banner flapping against the side of a building. She walked inside and asked to speak to a salesperson.

———

Sarah left the store after purchasing a burner phone and placed her first call. She listened to the various menu options—which, of course, had recently changed—and hit 0 to be connected to an operator.

"NYU School of Medicine."

"Hi. Do you know Dr. Paul Johansen?"

"Yes."

"I need to get him a message."

"Sure. Let me connect you."

"Wait. Can you just give him a written message?"

"I don't have time to play games," the woman said and hung up.

Sarah called back and re-entered her previous selections.

"NYU School of Medicine."

"Hi, my name is Dr. Sarah Brenalen. To whom am I speaking?"

"Andrea Warner, administrative coordinator."

"Andrea, please don't hang up. This is not a prank call. Paul's phones and computers have been hacked. I need you to give him a written message."

Andrea didn't respond, but neither did she hang up. That was a good sign. Without revealing details, Sarah was able to convince the skeptical administrative coordinator to hand Paul a note instructing him what to do.

"I get off work at five. I'll stop by his office and give him your message." Andrea said.

"Can't you do it sooner?"

"No. Paul works in another building."

"That's okay. Thank you for your help."

Sarah ended the call, thrust both fists triumphantly into the air, and took a minute to appreciate her accomplishments. Against all odds, she'd escaped and taken the money. By now, Marcel probably knew it. He would soon break into her home and find the two notes she'd written. Would they appease him? Regardless, Step One of her plan was officially in the books. And she would complete Step Two later this evening. Even if Andrea couldn't give Paul the message until 6:00 p.m. eastern time, she'd still have a couple of hours to talk to him and get to an FBI office before it closed. But which one?

She thought back to her computer-generated list of

Bay Area FBI offices and ruled out the one in San Jose. If Marcel feared she'd run to the Feds, that's the first place he'd stake out. The list also included an FBI office in downtown San Francisco. No. Marcel might send a hit-man—or hitwoman—over there because it was near the Bank of America branch that had just handed her two million dollars. The only other FBI office she remembered was in Concord—an East Bay city about thirty miles away. It seemed like her best bet. With more than four hours to kill before Paul called, she decided to take the subway to Concord, get something to eat, and check into a hotel.

Sarah ran one block to the Embarcadero BART station and boarded an Antioch-bound train. It was standing room only as she elbowed her way past an assortment of students, professionals, and a man clearly in need of psychiatric help. She commandeered a spot in the corner and stood with her backpack pressed against the wall.

The train completed its 3.6-mile-long journey beneath San Francisco Bay and emerged in Oakland. After two downtown stops, a seat became available. She sat down, hugged her backpack, and closed her eyes.

———

Sarah snapped awake as the BART train rolled into the Concord station. Her watch read 10:49 a.m. She got off the train, rode an escalator to street level, and walked through downtown—physically and mentally spent. And hungry. She stepped inside a Mexican restaurant and ordered huevos rancheros, a guacamole salad, and decaf coffee.

"Anything else?" the waitress asked.

"No. But I'm wondering if there's a hotel within walking distance?"

———

Sarah was incredulous. "You're telling me I can't pay in cash?"

"We require a credit card," the Hilton Concord manager informed her. "You don't have one?"

"Somebody stole it," she lied.

"I'm sorry, but that's our policy."

"So, what am I supposed to do? Sleep on the street?"

"I suggest you try the Comfort Inn."

She did. Same result.

After storming out of the Comfort Inn, she walked several blocks and came upon the Breezeway Motel. With its dingy façade and litter-strewn parking lot, it looked like the kind of place that rented rooms by the hour. Desperate for a bed, she decided to give it a shot.

Sarah entered the two-story motel and approached a man staffing the front desk. He seemed surprised when she requested a room—perhaps because she wasn't accompanied by a "kerb crawler." She told him her Visa card had been stolen and was relieved to hear his response: No credit card? No problem. "But you'll have to pay now," he added.

After checking into Room 104, she dropped her backpack on the bed and pulled out an expensive bottle of wine. It was intended to both celebrate her escape and calm frazzled nerves.

She fetched a plastic cup from the bathroom, uncorked the bottle of Cabernet Sauvignon, filled her cup and, without pausing to savor the bouquet, took a gulp.

After relishing a few more sips of wine, she called Cal Power and pressed number 3 for the maintenance department. A supervisor named Vince Hartman answered and told her Rogelio was out on a job.

"When he gets back, can you have him call me?"

"Sure."

She got Vince to write down her new phone number, and confirmed he'd written it correctly.

"Tell him it's urgent. And I know this sounds crazy, but I need him to use *your* office phone when he calls me."

"You want him to use *my* phone?"

"Yes. It's not a joke. His phone has been hacked. He must use *your* phone. Okay?"

"Okay. Got it."

"Thank you so much."

She ended the call and polished off the cup of wine. With no unfinished business left on her agenda, she took a hot shower and climbed into bed. Before closing her eyes, she made sure her new phone was next to the pillow.

———

Vince Hartman was operating a bandsaw in the maintenance shop when he saw Rogelio pull up in his truck and get out. "Hey, Ro. Your girlfriend called."

Rogelio looked at him. *"What?"*

"About a half-hour ago. She said—"

"Wait a minute. She called *you*?"

"Yeah. She wants you to use my phone and call her back."

"I don't need a third-party messenger service."

"Okay, I'm just telling you. She said it was important. Something about—"

"If it's that damn important, *she* can call *me*."

chapter thirteen

Sarah woke up to the sound of knocking. She raised her head off the pillow, glanced at her phone, and was shocked to see it was 5:41 p.m. Neither Paul nor Rogelio had called.

A second round of knocking was considerably louder. She turned on a light and squinted at the blurry hotel room door.

"Who's there?"

"Jon McFettridge from Homeland Security. I need to ask you a few questions."

She closed her eyes and tried to comprehend how they got involved.

"Ma'am?"

"Just a minute. I have to get dressed," she said and got out of bed.

As she slipped on her jeans and turtleneck, she wondered if her visitor was from Homeland Security. What if he was one of Marcel's men? But how could that be? She'd escaped them.

"I'm sorry, who are you again?"

"Jon McFettridge. Homeland Security."

"Hold on. I'm coming right now," she lied.

Unsure who was lurking on the other side of the door and realizing that Paul or Rogelio might call, she grabbed her phone, turned it off, and hid it under the mattress. She pulled the syringe of Entoryl-XT from her backpack and darted over to the hotel phone to dial 911. She heard the door open behind her. "Federal agent! Put your hands up!"

Sarah followed the man's order.

"What's that in your hand?"

"A syringe."

"Set it down *now*."

She complied.

"Good. Now I want you to place both hands on the top of your head and keep your back to me."

Sarah's heart raced as she interlocked the fingers of both hands behind her head and stared at the wall. She heard footsteps and sensed the man was now standing directly behind her.

"Now listen carefully. I'm going to frisk you. I'll do it as respectfully as I can."

She felt one of his hands travel from the top of her head to her neck and breasts, and down to her stomach, butt, inner thighs, and calves.

"Keep your hands where they are, do a one-eighty, and walk to the chair. Then you're going to sit down. Do you understand?"

"Yes." She turned around and gasped when she saw that the man was pointing a gun at her face. "Please put that down."

"I'll only discharge my firearm if necessary."

His partner, also holding a gun, was guarding the door. They were both young, clean-cut, and wearing conservative black suits. One would expect them to be wielding Bibles, not handguns.

"Go sit down," he ordered.

She took nervous steps and sat in the chair as directed.

"Now place your hands on the armrests and keep them there." He slid his gun into a holster inside his suit jacket and flipped open a wallet with a gold badge and identification card. "Again, I'm Special Agent Jon McFettridge." He turned his head toward the door. "And that's U.S. Marshal Collin Smith."

There was a knock at the door, and Collin opened it. Marcel walked into the room, and Sarah was immediately sick to her stomach.

Jon went over to the nightstand, picked up the syringe, and delivered it to Marcel. "She was holding this when we made our entry."

Marcel examined it, making sure a safety cap covered the needle's tip. "Be careful when handling this," he said and laid the syringe on the bureau. "Collin, I want you to thank the hotel manager for unlocking the door for us. Tell him everything's under control."

"Gotcha," he replied.

"And stay in the lobby in case someone heard commotion and called the police."

"Will do," he said and left the room.

"Jon, did you get her phone?" Marcel asked.

"She's not carrying one," he replied.

"Check her backpack."

"Sure, boss." Jon unzipped the main compartment of Sarah's backpack. He looked inside and froze when he saw two stacks of hundred-dollar bills.

"What's wrong?" Marcel asked.

"Nothing," he said and began a search.

"I left my phone at home," Sarah said. "It's in a drawer of my nightstand."

Jon completed his search. "I don't see one."

Marcel placed a call. "We have her. . . . Enter her house if you think it's safe to do so. . . . Yes, it would be useful to know how she escaped. . . . Okay, goodbye."

He walked over to Sarah and looked down at her. "Your rebellious nature is trying my patience. But, on the other hand, I admire your *compétence sous le feu.*"

He strode back to the bureau, raised the bottle of wine, and examined its label. "I also admire your taste in wines. If I'm forced to choose a California vintner, Caymus is a worthy selection. Would you care for some more?"

"Yes."

He poured a few ounces of wine into the plastic cup and held it out for her. She looked at Jon. "He told me I couldn't take my hands off the armrests."

Marcel smiled. "It's okay."

Sarah took the cup in her trembling right hand and sipped. "How did you find me?"

He sat on the edge of the bed and leaned toward her. "I thought I'd made it quite clear; we're very good at what we do. You're a decent runner, but you're no match for my surveillance team. I suspected you might remove the anklet, so we were more than prepared to follow you if you escaped."

"I had no choice. You were going to kill me."

Marcel chuckled. "Such a vivid imagination."

"You *accosted* me. I didn't imagine that," Sarah said. "And I still don't know who you are, or why you want my T-3."

"Okay. I suppose we owe you an explanation," he said. "I'm going to tell you the truth. I live in Paris and work for the *Direction du renseignement militaire*. I'm here to help your government carry out a mission."

"A *mission*?"

"Yes. I'm sure you've heard of the terrorist organization Jaysh Allah. We know of an underground bunker where its central leadership resides. Unfortunately, the bunker is in an urban area—approximately seven meters beneath a neighborhood where thousands of people live. So, bombing it is out of the question.

"We considered pumping carbon monoxide or a poisonous gas into the compound, but they've installed air monitors and would be alerted. Besides, we'd have no control over a gas once it's released. We could kill civilians.

"We even considered a ground assault," Marcel continued. "Unfortunately, the compound is heavily guarded and booby-trapped, so an attack would prove costly. And the men we're after could escape through a network of tunnels. So, while we've wanted to destroy this terrorist command center for some time, we had no plan.

"Then we learned of your drug."

Marcel stood and began pacing. "Sarah, do you realize how much bottled water they carry into that compound? What if we could inject T-3 into those bottles? It's possible that most of the leadership could be wiped out without firing a single shot. Without dropping one bomb. With no soldier or civilian casualties. That's why we contacted you."

Sarah looked up. "Then why didn't you tell me that in the first place?"

"Because we wanted to protect you."

She exhaled derisively.

"It's true," Marcel said. "Let's assume this mission is successful. We'd do our best to conceal your identity, but it could be leaked. If so, terrorists the world over would long to kidnap you. And if they succeeded? They'd grab you by your beautiful braids and saw off your head. Or throw you into a cage and set it alight.

"So, we chose a different ploy, albeit one more complicated. Now if our mission succeeds and your name is leaked, everyone will know you were coerced. You had no idea of the intended target. It could save your life."

Sarah shot him disdainful eyes. "You threatened to kill me, but I'm supposed to believe you wanted to save my life."

"I never aimed a rifle at your head. We just had to make sure you didn't inform anyone. Without absolute secrecy, this mission could be jeopardized. You must believe me."

"Then let me talk to someone at Homeland Security and see if they can vouch for you."

Marcel shook his head. "They couldn't do it. Neither Jon nor Collin is employed by your DHS. They work for a special, anti-terrorist task force that was created for this job."

"Bullshit," Sarah said.

Marcel shrugged. "Well, I guess I don't know what else to tell you."

He sat down on the edge of the bed, and his phone rang. He answered it and listened for several seconds before responding. "I agree. Jon and I will take her in my car. We should be there in four to five hours. Goodbye."

He reached down, picked up her shoes, and dropped them at her feet. "Put them on. We're leaving soon."

"Where are you taking me?"

He ignored her question and looked at Jon. "I'll be back shortly. I must speak with Collin." He walked to the hotel room door, hesitated, and turned to his partner. "Oh, and she may have all the wine she wants," he said and left the room.

Sarah took deep breaths and tried to convince herself that Marcel and his cohorts were anti-terrorist agents working for her government. But as she began to calm down, she considered the unthinkable: what if *they* were the terrorists?

She decided she had no choice but to attempt another escape. Of course, the odds of escaping a second time in one day were minuscule. Her physical and mental capacities were drained. And a man was holding her hostage.

Sarah looked at the door and figured she could reach it in three seconds. But three seconds seemed an eternity. She then remembered the syringe of Entoryl-XT. Was it still on the bureau?

She watched Jon walk over to the window. He parted the shades and looked outside. She put on her shoes, stood up, and took slow, deliberate steps toward the bureau. Jon whipped around. "Hey, I told you to stay in that chair."

She stopped and raised her empty cup. "I'm just getting some more wine. Marcel said it was okay."

Jon nodded an uneasy approval. "Okay. But if you run to the door or scream for help, those last four seconds of your life will be excruciatingly painful. *Comprende*?"

"Yes."

Sarah reached the bureau, and her heart skipped a beat when she saw the syringe. There it was. And within reach. But she sensed Jon's stare and decided to let it be. Instead, she grabbed the wine bottle and poured a small amount into her cup. On her way back to the chair, she spotted her black hoodie at the foot of the bed and picked it up.

"Hey! What do you think you're doing?" Jon barked.

"I'm cold."

He snatched it from her, searched the front pocket, and tossed it back.

"Thanks," she said and pulled it down over her head. She sat in the chair, raised the cup of wine to her lips, and pretended to sip.

Jon picked up his phone and began a texting session with someone. She noticed a pattern. He'd type a few words, look at her, type a few more words, send his text, and watch her until he received a reply. Then he'd begin a new message.

While Jon was preoccupied with his phone, she poured the wine between the arm of her chair and the seat cushion and got up for another trip to the bureau. Jon watched as she refilled her cup and went back to his phone. She set the bottle down, scooped up the syringe, and slid it into the front pocket of her hoodie. Jon typed a few characters and shot her another glance. He saw nothing that concerned him. She walked back to her seat.

Marcel returned a few minutes later and spoke indiscernible words to Jon. Whatever he said triggered a discussion—or more accurately, an argument—conducted in hushed voices. From her ringside seat, Sarah watched them go at it. With each back and forth, Marcel and Jon grew more agitated, and she could only hope their exchange of barbs would escalate into an exchange of bullets. Their slugfest continued but remained verbal and never reached decibel levels unsuitable for a library.

"Excuse me," she interjected.

They stopped jawing and looked at her.

"I need to use the restroom."

"Wait," Marcel said. He walked into the bathroom

and searched for any weapons or hazardous materials she might have hidden. He reappeared, brushed away dust that had collected on his pants while kneeling on the bathroom floor, and checked his watch. "Okay. You have five minutes."

Sarah walked into the bathroom, closed, and locked the door, and removed the syringe of Entoryl-XT from her hoodie pocket. While debating what to do next, she heard Marcel speak in an angry voice: "No, I didn't take it. I left it on the bureau." Jon's response was inaudible. She placed an ear against the bathroom door and listened.

"You let her get up and walk?"

"Don't blame me," Jon replied. "If you'd gotten rid of the syringe after—"

"No, no," Marcel snapped. "If you kept her confined to the chair, as you were supposed to do, we wouldn't have this problem."

"You said she could have all the wine she wanted."

"Yes. But I never implied she could get up and walk around."

A knock on the bathroom door startled her. "Sarah. I know you have the syringe," Marcel said. "I want you to place it on the floor and come out."

He backed away from the door and drew his gun. "You have ten seconds to come out."

"Why don't you come in?" Sarah replied dispassionately. "The door's unlocked."

"No, I'm not coming in."

"That's okay. I'm in no hurry. I'll just wait."

"Open the door, place the syringe on the floor, and come out *now*."

The door creaked open just enough to allow a fine outline of light on three sides. Marcel looked at Jon. "Get me a long stick or a broom," he whispered.

Jon left and returned with an ironing board. Marcel scoffed. "I don't need to press my trousers."

"This is a hotel room, not a fucking Home Depot. You find something better."

Marcel put his gun away and grabbed the ironing board. He extended it and prodded the door open another inch.

"Don't be afraid. I'm sitting on the floor against the wall," Sarah said.

Marcel coaxed the door open wide enough to confirm her statement. She was indeed sitting on the floor and leaning against a wall. The syringe was in her right hand and pointed at her left forearm.

"We're even. You have my T-3, and I have your two million dollars. Let me go."

"I'm afraid I can't do that," he said. "Now, put down the syringe and slide it across the floor to me."

"Let me go, or I'll inject myself. I swear to God I will."

"Sarah, listen to me. We're working for *your government*. We're not the enemy."

"Then why won't you let me call Homeland Security?"

"Because this is a classified operation. No one at the DHS—or, for that matter, the FBI or the CIA—knows anything about our mission."

"I don't believe you."

"Well then, what can I say?"

"Promise that if I inject myself, you'll drop me off at a hospital."

Marcel raised his hands in a conciliatory position. "You have my word."

"Then *say* it. I want to hear you say it."

"Okay. I promise that if you inject yourself, I'll take you to a hospital. But please don't do it. We need your help."

At that moment, Sarah jabbed the needle into her forearm and pushed the plunger. Marcel flung the ironing board and took two steps toward her. She removed the needle from her arm and dropped the empty syringe to the floor. Her head fell back against the wall, and her eyes lazily searched the ceiling before closing.

He crouched in front of her and shook her upper body. "Sarah."

Jon snickered. "That's a trip."

"Shut up, you fool," Marcel said. He studied Sarah's face and then grabbed her left wrist. He squeezed his other hand around her baby finger and bent it back until it was at a right angle. He bent it a few degrees more and heard a pop. Her expression didn't change.

"What are you doing?" Jon asked.

"I had to make sure she's not faking it," Marcel replied. He laid her hand down, walked out of the bathroom, and placed a call. "I have good news. Sarah injected herself with T-3. We're bringing her in." He turned to his partner. "You stay with her. I'm going to speak with Collin."

Marcel left, and Jon went over to the bed. He unzipped

Sarah's backpack, grabbed one of the stacks of hundred dollar bills, and stuffed it into a suit jacket pocket.

He was standing just outside the bathroom door and looking at Sarah when Marcel returned.

"Collin is moving my car. Are you ready?"

"Yeah, let's do it," he replied, and slung Sarah's backpack over his shoulder. The two men hoisted Sarah off the bathroom floor and maneuvered her past the bed. Collin appeared at the door. "It's clear. Hurry."

They carried Sarah down the hallway, out a rear exit, and placed her in the back seat of Marcel's rental car. Jon tossed the backpack next to her, closed the door, and got into the front passenger seat.

Marcel saw Collin backing up his car and called out to him. Collin lowered his window. "Yeah?"

"I want you to follow us back."

"Why?"

"It's best we stick together."

chapter fourteen

———

*A*n offshore storm was headed for Northern California. Marcel had heard that the first offerings of the rainy season made for slick roads and increased car accidents. A car accident could be their undoing, so he wanted to get to his destination before the atmospheric river unleashed its fury. But he stuck to the speed limit. He couldn't risk a ticket or any questions a nosy highway patrol officer might ask about the unresponsive woman in the back seat.

Jon, who'd been surprisingly quiet since they left the Breezeway Motel, turned around and eyed Sarah. "So, what's the deal with this drug?"

Marcel checked the speedometer again.

"Talk to me. Is she brain-dead?"

"Her drug destroys everything but the most basic functions necessary to sustain life."

"Wow," Jon said. "Do you realize that when I went

into her room, she was locked and loaded? She was going to inject *me* with that shit."

Yes. And it's a shame she didn't, Marcel thought but didn't verbalize. His phone rang, and he answered the call. He listened for several seconds before speaking.

"Interesting. . . . Good. . . . Yes, it's imperative you leave the letter she wrote to her boyfriend. He's coming over to her house Friday evening. If he doesn't see it, he might go to the police. . . . I agree. . . . Okay, goodbye."

He slid his phone back into a suit jacket pocket and drove on without saying a word. Jon's curiosity got the better of him, as Marcel knew it would. "Okay, so who called?"

"Sam. He led the entry into Sarah's home. They discovered how she was able to escape. They also found two notes she left behind. One to her boyfriend and one to me."

"Ooh, a perfumed note just for you. What did it say?"

"She feared we would kill her, so she decided to take the two million dollars and run. She wasn't going to tell the authorities and, in exchange, asked that we leave her alone."

"That's it? Nothing about how she has the hots for you?"

Marcel ignored his partner and checked the rearview mirror. Headlights from passing cars illuminated Sarah's face. She was motionless. Expressionless.

The two men, mindful of their caustic relationship and the long drive ahead, went several minutes without speaking. Eventually, Jon broke the silence. "Shit!" he blurted out.

Marcel flinched. "What's wrong?"

"I'm missing the damn game. Do you mind if I listen to it?" Jon asked. He turned on the radio before getting a response and tapped through the FM spectrum until he found what he was searching for:

"Swing, and there's a high fly ball to medium center field. Perez barely has to move. He makes the catch, and Elsberry is retired for the second out. That will bring up . . ."

Jon lowered the radio volume. "Hey, old man, do you like baseball?"

"No."

"This is Giants and Padres. They're tied for first place in the NL West."

The designated hitter struck out to end the inning, and an animated voice began trumpeting the bargains at Toyota of Fremont.

Jon again turned to the back seat. This time he ogled Sarah for several seconds. "Hey, you know what I'm thinking. How about we stop at a motel for an hour. Wouldn't that be cool? I mean, she's not bad looking. Nice body. It would be like one of those date-rape drugs. Nobody will know. What do you say?"

He waited in vain for a response. "C'mon, what do you say?"

"You're a despicable human being."

Jon laughed. "Really? You practically ripped her finger off, but *I'm* despicable?"

"Again, I had to make sure she wasn't faking it."

"And obviously, she isn't. Let's take her to a motel and have some fun."

"You disgust me."

"Don't give me that self-righteous bullshit. You know you'd like to do her. Hell, I'll even let you go first."

They drove on without further words until passing a sign that promised gas, food, and lodging in one mile. Jon eyed Marcel expectantly. "Let's do it. It's not like she's going to tell anyone."

Marcel flipped the turn signal, and a green dash-board light and clicking sound pulsated in unison. He took the exit and came to a stop at the bottom of the off-ramp. A right turn onto Mason Road delivered them to what Jon thought was their destination: the Best Western Motel. His eager anticipation gave way to puz-zlement as Marcel drove past the motel and through an Exxon station before pulling into a remote spot in the parking lot of Lenka's Family Restaurant.

"Why'd you park here?" Jon asked.

Marcel turned and looked out the back window. "I thought Collin was following us."

"Okay, I'll try again. Why'd you park here?"

"I need a cup of coffee, and I want her away from public view."

"Then we're going to the motel?"

"No."

"Aah, man. Don't do this to me."

"I need you to stay with her. Can I get you some-thing?"

"No, I'm good," Jon replied as he increased the play-by-play volume of the ballgame. "Just one thing."

"Yes?"

"If we're not here when you get back, check the Best Western."

Marcel ached to pump a few bullets into the guy. Instead, he got out of the car and thrust a finger at Jon. "Don't you so much as touch her."

Jon slapped his hand away. "I'm kidding, okay? Go get your fucking coffee."

Marcel slammed the door shut, walked the entire length of the parking lot, and entered the restaurant. Jon pulled the stack of bills from his suit jacket pocket and fanned it. Distant lights provided enough illumination for him to verify that all of them had the number 100 in the upper left corner. "I guess I got the last laugh, you old bastard."

He removed the paper band and began counting the bills on his lap. He became so engrossed in his newfound wealth that he didn't register the three-run double by Cesar Chacon that gave the Giants a seven to five lead over the Padres. He didn't even notice the first drops of rain that made their mark on the windshield as the storm worked its way inland from the Pacific Ocean. Nor did he see the human form rising up behind him in the back seat. He did, however, feel the sharp sting in his Adam's apple and the excruciating pain that welled over him as a shiny knife, gripped tightly in this smooth hand, twisted deeper into his throat. And he did notice the liquid spurting out of the hole below his chin, splattering ruby red droplets onto his pile of hundred-dollar bills.

Sarah let go of the knife and jumped out of the car

as Jon clutched his throat and belched a gurgling sound. To her surprise, he swung open the front passenger-side door and staggered out. His pile of money fell onto the pavement and began scattering in the breeze. He tried to tackle her, but she raced around the car and got into the driver's seat. Before she could start the engine, he lunged back inside and grabbed her by the hair with his left hand. She screamed and pried at his fingers. He let go of his throat, pulled a gun from its holster, and pressed it against her forehead. She instinctively gripped the barrel and silencer, pointed it away, and sunk her teeth into his right thumb. Jon moaned and fired two shots through the driver's door before surrendering the weapon. He again cupped his throat with his right hand while maintaining an ironclad grip on her hair with his left. She coiled her elbow and delivered two blows to his face. He grimaced and howled unintelligible words as blood trickled from his shattered nose. She reared back and gave him another *Empi Uchi* that rocked him sideways. His left hand went limp.

Sarah grabbed her backpack, ran from the car, and slid down an embankment. Intense pain was coming from her left hand and right elbow, but she couldn't worry about that right now. She instead focused on her fight with Jon. Had she killed him? It was unconscionable. But what if he wasn't dead? Was that a good thing? There was still a loaded gun in the car. And what about Marcel? He'd soon return and track her down. She trudged through mud, knee-deep weeds, and assorted trash before stopping at what was hopefully a safe vantage point.

She clawed her way up to ground level and could see Marcel's BMW. Three doors were open, the interior lights on. And there was Jon, crawling the wet pavement in an attempt to retrieve the elusive hundred-dollar bills. An SUV approached the surreal scene, and Jon was now center stage in its headlamps. The vehicle came to a stop, but no one got out. Its windshield wipers swished away raindrops. Jon shot a hand skyward, perhaps pleading for help, or begging not to be run over. A female driver finally emerged from the SUV and ran to his aid.

Sarah bolted for the restaurant with her backpack bouncing off her spine. Twenty feet from the entrance, she crouched behind a truck and waited for Marcel to appear. It was not a long wait. He exited the restaurant, stopped for a moment, and then dropped his takeout coffee and ran toward the commotion.

Marcel reached the crime scene and saw a woman hunched over Jon. She looked up at him. "I don't know what happened, but he's bleeding real bad. I called nine-one-one."

Marcel crouched beside her. "He's my friend. And I'm a doctor. Let me take over."

"Please."

"And could you do me a favor?" He pointed at the hundred-dollar bills scattered on the ground. "Could you retrieve his money?"

"Sure."

Marcel rolled Jon onto his back and recoiled. His face was a pulpy, red mess. He gasped short, irregular breaths, and his eyes were indicative of a man who'd just experienced living hell. He pried Jon's hands away from his neck and examined the injury. Neither of his carotid arteries was severed. He removed a handkerchief from his breast pocket and pressed it against the wound. "You're one lucky son of a bitch."

Jon tried to move, but Marcel restrained him. "Lie still." He looked up and watched the woman collect the bills. Satisfied that she was performing her task, he glared at Jon. "I leave you for five minutes—literally *five minutes*—and you let Sarah escape."

"I think I got all of it," the woman said, holding a bedraggled pile of hundred-dollar bills.

"Thank you. I warned him not to carry so much money. It only invites trouble." He took the pile from her and peeled two hundreds off the top. "Here. This is for you. You've been a big help."

The woman shook her head. "I don't need a reward. I just want to make sure he's okay."

"He'll be fine. Now please take this and go."

She hesitated, accepted the money, and walked to her car.

Marcel heard a distant siren. "We must get out of here," he whispered to Jon, and began helping him to his feet.

The woman turned around. "What are you doing? Wait for the ambulance."

A man appeared and grabbed Marcel's right bicep with a firm hand. "Do not move him."

"He's okay."

"Sir, I'm a volunteer EMT, and I insist."

"And I'm a doctor," Marcel shot back. "He's breathing on his own. His carotids are not damaged. It looks worse than it is."

"You may be right. But let's lay him down on his side so that blood doesn't drain into his lungs."

Marcel decided not to challenge him further and acquiesced. The two lowered Jon to the pavement. The man took off his coat, covered Jon's upper body with it, and patted his shoulder. "Hey, buddy. An ambulance will be here in a minute. Just relax. You're going to be okay."

As the man spoke comforting words, Marcel reached inside Jon's pocket and removed his wallet. He got up, took several steps across the blacktop, and called Collin Smith.

"Where are you?"

"I'm on 101."

"I asked you to follow me," Marcel admonished.

"I did. But I got tired of driving fifty miles an hour. Why? Is there a problem?"

"No. There are *three* problems: Sarah escaped, Jon's injured, and the police are coming."

chapter fifteen

Sarah swooped inside Lenka's Family Restaurant and noticed an elderly couple talking to the cashier. They turned to leave, and she ran over to them.

"Excuse me," she said between labored breaths. "Do you think I could catch a ride with you?"

They gawked at her and shuffled away without saying a word. She noted their frightened expressions and knew something was wrong. Very wrong.

She jogged into the women's restroom and headed to a mirror fronting two sinks. She was not prepared for the sight. Her face and clothes were splattered with fresh blood. Red globules clung to her hair. She ran into the stall and hunched over the toilet.

The restroom door opened, and she spun around and locked the stall. She heard the click of high heels on linoleum but saw nothing through her narrow view of the outside. She no longer had a syringe of Entoryl-XT or a knife and looked for something sharp. A piece of metal. Anything. She slid a ring of keys from her pants pocket and gripped the longest one in an outstretched hand. She heard the trickle of a water faucet. The ratcheting of a paper towel dispenser. More footsteps. The restroom door opened and closed, and all was quiet again. She unlatched the stall door and poked her head out. The coast was clear.

Back at the sink, Sarah pulled her shoes off and saw clumps of mud that had collected during her run through the drainage ditch. She took off her blood-stained hoodie, jeans, and turtleneck, and stuffed them into a trashcan. She then scrubbed her hands and face and rinsed her hair until the last of the reddish-hued water had swirled down the drain. Free of Jon's blood, she dried herself with paper towels, grabbed a fresh pair of pants and a top from her backpack, and put them on.

Her left hand was crying out for help. While anxious to leave, she held it under a stream of cold water and experienced immediate relief. She watched the water flow over her swollen joint and knew that Marcel had definitively answered one question. He was not her friend.

She picked up her mud-caked shoes, held them over the trashcan, and clapped the soles together. After putting them on, she conducted a final inspection in the mirror. All looked good. It was time to go.

Sarah inched open the restroom door, saw no enemies, and walked quickly into the dining room. She noticed two young men getting up from a booth and hurried over to them. "Excuse me, are you guys leaving?"

The taller of the two, a skinny twenty-something, gave her a curious look. "Yeah, why?"

"Can I catch a ride with you?"

Neither of them responded.

"Please. I got stranded here."

"What happened?" asked the shorter, stockier one. "Your car broke down?"

She looked around the restaurant while trying to invent a believable story. "My boyfriend and I were driving to Sacramento and got into an argument. We pulled in here to get gas and, next thing I knew, he drove off without me."

"*Seriously?*" the shorter one asked.

"I thought he'd come back, but that was two hours ago."

"Did you call him?"

"He's not answering his phone. Look, I was going to get an Uber, but I'll give you a hundred dollars for a ride to BART or Caltrain. What do you say?"

"Sure," the stocky one said. He nodded at his friend. "But first I gotta drop him off at the airport."

"That's fine. Can we go?"

"After I take care of some business," he replied and headed to the restroom.

While mentally imploring him to hurry the hell up, Sarah detected the faint wailing of an emergency vehicle. Then a second siren and possibly a third. The sirens grew louder and soon matched in volume the dreary, instrumental version of *Yesterday* that oozed from the restaurant sound system.

"You ready?" the tall one asked.

"Yeah."

They started walking to the exit but stopped in their tracks when they saw the spectacle of rotating beacons and flashers in the parking lot. Red, white, and blue lights ricocheted off the wet pavement, creating a mesmerizing light show on the restaurant's rain-spattered windows.

He turned to her. "I wonder what that's all about."

"I don't know."

"By the way, I'm Chris. What's your name?"

"Sarah."

"Nice to meet you. My friend's name is Damien—like that little freak in the *Omen* movies. He's taking me to the airport. I'm flying back to LA."

"Which airport?" she asked.

"LAX."

"No, I mean which airport is he taking you to?"

"Oh. San Jose."

Damien emerged from the restroom and caught up with Chris and Sarah, who were still focused on the emergency vehicles in the parking lot. He smirked. "I'm telling you; these rest-stop drive-by shootings are getting out of hand."

"No shit," Chris said. "I won't feel safe 'til I get back to Compton."

They proceeded to the exit, stepped outside into a light drizzle, and walked to a Camaro Coupe. Damien opened the driver's door and let Sarah get into the back seat. He got behind the wheel, unlocked the front passenger door, and Chris got in.

"I don't know about you, but I'm curious," Damien said. He started the engine and drove toward the flashing lights.

They neared the accident scene, and Sarah saw paramedics attending to Jon, who lay face up on the ground. A police officer was talking to the woman who'd stopped to help. And there was Marcel, holding court with another officer.

An idea came to her: This might be a good time to take him down. She could jump out of the car and scream that he'd assaulted her. Unfortunately, none of the police officers would have a clue what she was talking about. Meanwhile, the professional hitman could pull out his silver-plated handgun and start shooting. She decided not to risk any lives.

The Camaro drew close—perhaps too close—and an agitated cop ran over and motioned for Damien to back off. That caught Marcel's attention, and he looked at the car. It was too late to hide. He homed in on her, and she froze. Their eyes locked. Two heavyweights before the title fight.

As ordered, Damien backed up the car. Marcel rotated his head to maintain eye contact with her while continuing to talk to the policeman. He appeared unflustered, confident she wouldn't break his cover. And conversely, he made no attempt to stop her getaway. Theirs was an unspoken truce; they would settle their score another day.

Damien completed a semi-circle around the crime scene and drove off. Sarah looked out the back window and watched the flashing lights grow small and disappear.

"Here's my take on it," Damien said as he got onto the highway. "Mr. Prone—the man receiving CPR—was headed to the restaurant to grab a burger. He was yappin' on *his* cell phone and not paying attention to where he was walking. Meanwhile, June Cleaver—the woman talking to the cop—was yappin' on *her* cell phone and not paying attention to where she was driving. So, Mr. Prone had an unexpected encounter with the grille of Mrs. Cleaver's SUV. What do you think?"

Chris high-fived him. "I think you got it, Sherlock."

"And my dear Watson, do you see the moral in this story?"

"Yeah. Don't fuck with Mrs. Cleaver," Chris replied.

The two enjoyed a laugh, but Sarah was not amused. She leaned forward. "Excuse me, do either of you have any pain medication?"

Chris turned to her. "Damien's got some medical marijuana. It's guaranteed to relieve pain. You want to try some?"

"No thanks. That's okay," Sarah replied and slumped back down. She closed her eyes, elevated her left hand, and cursed.

How did they find me?

She remembered ditching the anklet and sprinting to the Redwood City Caltrain station. She reached the boarding platform as an express train was pulling in. It departed within a minute. After arriving in San Francisco, she ran a crisscross route to the bank—along the way ducking into office buildings through main entrances and leaving through side doors. By the time she walked into the Bank of America, she was damn sure no one was following her.

But she was wrong. They'd followed her from Redwood City to Room 104 of the Breezeway Motel.

"How?" she whispered.

Unable to answer that question, she focused on the positive: she'd just escaped a second time. But was she free?

Three men had taken her hostage. Hopefully, Marcel was still talking to the police. Jon was either on his way to a hospital or the morgue. That left Collin. Unfortunately, she had no clue as to his whereabouts.

She looked out the back window at a glittering display of automobile headlights and feared he was on her tail. She considered asking Damien to pull over to the side of the freeway. She could jump out of the car and run. It seemed like a good plan. But the thought of being alone and running for her life on a cold, drizzly night produced a knot in her stomach.

"You flying Southwest?" Damien asked his friend as he flipped the turn signal and took the exit for San Jose International Airport.

"Yeah," Chris replied. "Terminal B."

Sarah listened to their exchange and came up with an interesting idea: why not get out here and catch a flight? Not only would the San Jose airport offer a haven, one flight would whisk her away from danger. And if she saw Collin boarding the same plane, she could alert the crew.

Sarah sat up in her seat and saw the gleaming airport terminal just ahead.

"Hey, it's been real," Chris said.

"Dude, thanks for coming," Damien replied. "I'll try and make it down to SoCal next spring."

"Do it, bro. Come on down."

Damien maneuvered his Camaro over to the passenger drop-off curb, and he and Chris jumped out. Sarah pulled herself out of the back seat and saw the young men exchanging a hug and a few words. She extended two hundred-dollar bills toward Damien. "Thanks. I'm getting out here."

He stared in disbelief. "You don't have to pay me."

"Please. Take it."

Sarah ran into the terminal and saw people lined up at the Southwest, British Airways, and Cathay Pacific check-in counters. She then spotted a ticket agent standing behind a counter with no customers. She went over and was immediately summoned by the agent.

"Hi. When's your next flight?" Sarah asked.

"To where?"

"It doesn't matter."

The agent gave her a surprised look. "Okay. Our next flight is to Paris. It departs at 9:55. Arrives at Charles de Gaulle Airport at 5:40 p.m. tomorrow."

Unbelievable. Un-fucking believable. What were the chances her best shot to escape Marcel was a flight to his hometown? But what was the alternative? Her priority was to get out of San Jose. And besides, Paris was the last place on Earth he'd expect her to go.

"Are there any available seats?"

The agent looked at her monitor. "I show seven. But you'll have to hurry. Boarding has already begun."

"No problem. Can I pay you in cash?"

"Uh . . . sure," the agent replied, now wondering if she should call security. She completed the transaction and handed Sarah a paper ticket.

Sarah ran to passenger screening, handed her ticket and passport to a TSA agent, and joined a procession that crept forward. With each step, she examined her throbbing hand, checked the time, and looked for Collin or Marcel.

Nearing the security checkpoint, an agent reminded passengers to remove their shoes, belts, jewelry, and all items from their pockets before entering one of the body scanners.

Sarah followed his instructions and put her belongings in a plastic tub. She pushed it into the x-ray machine and made a successful trip through the scanner.

She saw an agent scrutinizing someone's luggage on a monitor and worried that the money in her backpack was piquing his interest. With the final minutes ticking away before her flight's scheduled departure, the x-ray machine spit out the gray container.

She collected her possessions, ran over to a chair, and sat down. While putting on her left shoe, she noticed a tiny, black object dangling near the heel and removed it. Her emotional roller coaster suddenly took another plunge into the depths of terror. It had three barbed legs.

She feverishly slipped on her shoes and had just tied the laces when a woman sat down beside her and placed a small shopping bag between them. It was neither gold colored nor from Neiman Marcus, but she nonetheless peeked inside: A box of Ghirardelli chocolates, a paperback novel, and a copy of *The Wall Street Journal*. No silver-plated handgun.

"Excuse me. May I ask where you're going?" Sarah asked.

The woman appeared to be taken aback by her question. "I'm flying to Singapore on business. Why?"

"Just curious."

Sarah discreetly dropped the transmitter into her bag and stood up. "Have a nice trip."

She began running to Gate 35 but stopped to consider something: why not go to the Homeland Security office at the airport? She'd just found a second GPS transmitter, and it would soon be on its way to Singapore. But there was a potential problem. What if Marcel had planted a third transmitter on her body? If so, going to the Feds would put Paul and Rogelio in danger. It wasn't worth the risk.

She ran all the way to deserted Gate 35, handed her ticket to the EuropeAir agent for processing, and continued down the jetway and onto the aircraft. Almost everyone was seated, so she walked unencumbered to row twenty-seven. She stuffed her backpack into an overhead storage bin and tapped a flight attendant on her shoulder.

"Excuse me. When you get a chance, could you get me some pain meds and a cup of water? I just broke my finger." She held up her swollen hand for good measure.

The flight attendant gawked. "Ouch. That looks bad."

"It hurts like hell."

"I can imagine. I'll be right back."

"Thanks," Sarah said and settled in between two passengers.

"Damn, I thought I was going to have an empty seat next to me," said the man to her right.

"Sorry."

"Just kidding. I usually get stuck next to some big fat guy, so you're fine."

She noticed that he was reading *Essential France*, and for the first time, it sunk in that she was actually on a plane bound for Paris. Of course, this was not how she envisioned her first trip. She should be bubbling over with excitement. And Rogelio should be sitting next to her. Instead, she was alone, nursing a broken finger, physically and emotionally drained, and fearing for her life.

The flight attendant returned and handed her a container of Tylenol and a bottled water. She then extended a box of gauze pads and a roll of surgical tape. "I think you should wrap your pinkie and ring finger together. It'll help stabilize the injury."

"Good idea. Thank you," Sarah said, accepting the supplies. She swallowed two pills with a gulp of water, stared at the erupting bruise on her left hand, and closed her eyes.

Marcel. You low-life piece of shit.

She remembered sitting on the bathroom floor in her
hotel room and injecting herself with Entoryl-XT. Marcel
crouched in front of her and said words that didn't register. The room spun, went black, and she was floating on a
cloud.

And then, just like that, the hallucinogenic effect of
Entoryl-XT dissipated and slapped her back to Earth. She
felt discomfort at the base of her left pinkie and heard a
conversation between two men. Barely cracking open her
eyes, she saw that she was riding in the back seat of a car.
Marcel and Jon were driving her somewhere.

The inexplicable pain began to increase at a worri-
some rate, and she used every ounce of willpower to ig-
nore it. She listened to Jon's rape fantasy and heard Marcel explain that he'd broken her finger to make sure she
wasn't faking it. Having gone from mellow to homicidal
in twenty seconds, she ached to sit up and rip their eye-
balls out. Instead, she focused on an important fact: They
believed she was brain-dead. Advantage Sarah.

With her hand screaming for attention, survival mode
kicked in. She thought about victims of mass shootings
who pretend to be dead—sometimes while lying in the
blood and brain matter of loved ones. In comparison, her
task seemed relatively easy: Don't grimace. Don't move. If
she could tolerate this pain for a few more minutes, she'd
get revenge. But how? She'd already used the syringe of
Entoryl-XT. And the T-3 was in a vial.

Then she remembered the knife tucked away in a
side pocket of her backpack. Yes, the knife. It was small

but very sharp. And within reach. She mentally prepared for combat. Then—

"This is a nonstop flight to Paris," came a voice over the intercom. "If Paris is not your destination, please leave the aircraft now." The announcement was repeated in French.

Sarah opened her eyes and looked at her watch. It was 10:07 p.m.—twelve minutes past the scheduled departure time. She wrapped the injured pinkie and taped it to her ring finger.

Five additional minutes passed. The plane still hadn't backed an inch away from the gate, and she worried that Marcel was responsible for the delay. She leaned forward and glared at a seatback, a mere two inches from her face.

Growing claustrophobic, she lifted herself up and surveyed the cabin. All passengers were settled in. Many were tinkering with their in-flight entertainment screen or some other electronic device. A few were engaged in conversation. A young, doe-eyed couple three rows back joined hands and shared a kiss. She envied—no, resented—their excitement.

She eased back down into her confined space. Her heel uncontrollably tapped the floor. A hand grabbed her shoulder, and she shrieked.

"Sorry to startle you," her favorite flight attendant said, "but you have to fasten your seatbelt for takeoff."

"Huh? Oh. Okay. Sure." Sarah clipped the two ends together and pulled it snug. "Are we leaving soon?"

"The ground crew is just now finishing up. We'll be taxiing shortly," she replied. "How's your finger?"

Sarah held up her left hand for an inspection. "Thanks to you, it's stabilized. Now, if the Tylenol would kick in."

"It will. Give it a minute."

The flight attendant continued down the aisle, making sure all passengers were buckled up, and then returned to check on Sarah. "You doing okay? You seem a bit anxious."

"Yeah. I guess I am."

"Tell you what. Once we hit cruising altitude, I'll page for a doctor."

Sarah shook her head. "No, no. It's okay. Really. I'm not worried about my finger. I just have a lot of stress in my life right now."

The flight attendant offered a concerned face. "That's not good."

"No. It's been a really tough week."

"I'm so sorry. Is that why you're going to Paris?"

"Yup."

She broke a smile. "Good. Sometimes it helps to get away."

Sarah nodded. "You got that right."

chapter sixteen

———

Collin Smith drove into the parking lot of Lenka's Family Restaurant, squeezed the brakes, and looked around. The rain had stopped—at least for the time being—but puddles of water covered much of the black pavement. He focused his eyes and saw in the distance two people standing near a couple of vehicles. He nudged the accelerator and proceeded in their direction. His headlamps soon illuminated two men. One was Marcel. The other was a police officer.

"You gotta be kidding me."

He drove a bit farther, parked, and stepped out of his car.

"Thank you for coming," Marcel said. "Officer Relei, this is my friend Collin Smith."

He looked at Collin and laughed. "What's with the matching suits? Were the three of you ushers at a wedding?"

Marcel ignored him and turned to Collin. "Jon was assaulted and robbed. He has a broken nose and a gash in his neck."

"*What?* Is he gonna be okay?"

"He won't be as loquacious for a while, but he'll recover."

"Gentlemen, I have to file my report," the officer said. "Take this as a lesson. Don't carry a lot of cash. Everyone accepts plastic these days."

"I couldn't agree with you more," Marcel said, and watched him get into his car and drive off. "Quick. Get your tablet and come with me."

He got behind the wheel of his BMW and started the engine. Collin hopped in the passenger seat and Marcel accelerated through the parking lot.

"Don't tell me," Collin said as he fired up his iPad, "Sarah attacked Jon and escaped."

"Yes."

"How the hell did that happen?"

"I don't know. I was in the restaurant getting carry-out. When I returned, Jon was lying on the ground. He was bleeding and in shock."

"Holy shit," Collin exclaimed. "She really fucked him up."

"Yes."

"That's crazy. I mean, Jon's a big boy."

"Apparently Sarah is very strong."

"And not real happy," Collin added.

"She also left behind a substantial amount of money. A mocking 'thank you' tip, I presume."

Collin looked at his iPad screen. "She's on Highway 101, six miles north of here."

"That would seem right. She escaped about ten minutes ago."

"You saw her get away?"

"She was in a car with two men. Unfortunately, I could do nothing to stop her."

Collin scrunched his eyebrows. "Wait a minute. How could she escape? She injected herself with T-3."

"Or so we thought," Marcel said. He made a left turn onto the highway entrance ramp. "It was probably an anesthetic that temporarily knocked her out."

"An anesthetic?"

"That's my guess. It would explain why she wanted me to drop her off at a hospital."

Collin nodded. "Now that's ingenious."

"Yes, it is. She's extremely intelligent."

"Intelligent, strong, *and* pissed off."

"Underestimate her at your peril," Marcel said.

They drove north on Highway 101, listening to raindrops and windshield wipers. Collin rechecked his screen. "I think she's going to the San Jose airport."

"Are you sure?"

"No, but the car she's in is headed in that direction."

"Then we don't have much time," Marcel said and upped his speed. He passed one car, moved over into the right-hand lane to pass two more cars, and then swerved back into the left lane.

"Hey!" Collin protested. "You keep driving like that, and this car will last us a lifetime."

"What do you mean?"

"It was a joke. But seriously, you're doing eighty-one miles an hour. And you're weaving in and out of traffic on a wet road. You keep it up, and we're both going to die."

Marcel didn't respond but eased up on the accelerator and slowed down to seventy-five.

"She's almost at the airport," Collin said. He turned to his partner. "I'm guessing you want to stop her before she gets on a plane."

"Yes."

"How do you plan to get past security?"

"I'll use my badge."

"Mmm, I wouldn't try it. It's one thing to bullshit a manager at some sleazy motel. But now you're going into an international airport that's crawling with security. And you speak with an accent. Someone's bound to check your credentials. You'll get busted."

"Then what do you suggest?"

"Buy a plane ticket, get through security, and hopefully you can find her. If not, don't worry about it. She isn't a threat right now anyway."

Collin gave Marcel directions to the San Jose airport, and within a few minutes they approached an impressive glass and steel structure.

"Where is she now?" Marcel asked.

"Terminal B."

They reached the terminal, and Marcel screeched to a stop behind an SUV unloading passengers and their suitcases. "I'll meet you back here."

"Good luck. And be careful."

Both men exited the car. Collin circled around the front and got into the driver's seat. Marcel ran inside Terminal B and saw a ticket agent standing behind a counter with no waiting line.

———

Jamee Kough processed her final customer—the woman who didn't care where she was going—and saw a Southwest agent. "Excuse me. You got a second?"

"Sure," the agent said and came over to her counter.

"A woman just asked me if she could buy a one-way ticket. To anywhere. Didn't matter. And she wanted to pay in cash. I wasn't sure what to do, so I sold her a ticket to Paris. Do you think I should call security?"

"Yes."

"I was going to, but then I thought: if she's a terrorist, she's not going to draw attention to herself."

"What if she's not a terrorist? What if she's mentally ill? Or suicidal?"

Jamee pursed her lips. "I hadn't thought of that."

"I think you should call security. They might want to ask her a few questions."

"Good idea."

"It's probably nothing, but you never know."

The Southwest agent smiled and walked away. As Jamee reached for the phone, a voice startled her: "Can you sell me a ticket?"

She snapped her head toward a man who'd just appeared at her counter. He was an older gentleman wearing a three-piece suit.

"Maybe," she replied. "That all depends on where you want to go."

Marcel shrugged. "I don't care. Anywhere is fine."

Jamee laughed. "Okay, what's going on?"

"What do you mean?"

"A woman came by here a few minutes ago and said the same thing."

"Interesting. Was she approximately thirty years old? Long braids?"

"That's her."

Marcel smiled.

She gave him a sly look. "Are the two of you playing some kind of a game?"

"It's a competition," he replied.

"Well, that would explain it." She looked at her monitor. "Unfortunately, you're too late for the Paris flight. Boarding closes in a few minutes."

"Just my luck. Thank you."

Marcel left Terminal B and searched a steady stream of vehicles for his rental car. In less than a minute, he saw the silver BMW and waved a hand in the air. Collin pulled over to the curb, and he got into the front passenger seat.

"That was quick," Collin said as he maneuvered past an idling van.

"I decided not to pursue her inside the airport. Too many cameras. Too much security."

"I agree. And she's not spilling her guts to anyone, so what's the rush?" Collin pointed out. "Besides, she's flying to Singapore. I've always wanted to go there."

Marcel gave him a confused look. "What are you talking about? She's flying to Paris."

"*Au contraire, mon chaud papillon.* Check out my tablet—Sarah's at Gate 26. And if you scroll to the next page, you'll see a 10:05 departure. It's going to Singapore."

"I don't care what your tablet is showing," Marcel countered. "I just spoke to an agent who sold her a ticket to Paris."

"Singapore. Paris. Whatever. Right now, I just want to know where I'm driving."

"Let's go back to the parking lot and retrieve your car," Marcel said. He pulled out his phone and made a call.

"Good morning. Are you enjoying retirement? . . . I apologize for waking you up, but I need your assistance. A EuropeAir flight from San Jose, California, to Paris should be departing soon. I want you to be at CDG when it arrives. Can you do that? . . . I'm looking for a woman who might be on the flight. . . . Great, I'll email her photo. . . . Thank you, Carlos. . . . Yes, I promise you a bottle of Henri IV Dudognon."

Marcel ended the call. "That was a former colleague of mine. He'll go to the airport and follow her if she arrives in Paris."

Collin drove into the parking lot of Lenka's Family Restaurant and spotted his car. "Unbelievable. It's still there. And I count four tires."

Marcel looked at his watch. "I don't know about you, but I'm a bit peckish. We have a long drive ahead, and it's getting late. Perhaps we should eat now."

"Sounds good to me," Collin said and parked the car.

They entered the restaurant, picked out a booth, and sat down. Marcel remembered coming here earlier to get a cup of coffee. At the time, he never would have imagined the events that had just unfolded.

A middle-aged waitress came by with two menus. After careful consideration, they each placed an order. She scribbled on a notepad, and Marcel gazed up at her.

"Are you closing soon?"

"No. We're open until one."

He flashed a charming smile. "Good. I want to enjoy my dining experience at your lovely *salle à manger*."

The waitress blushed and seemed at a loss for words. "I . . . sure. Thank you." She collected their menus and sashayed away.

"I have no idea what you just said, but you definitely made her day," Collin said.

The sky opened up, and Marcel watched torrents of water pummel the parking lot on the other side of the window. "I've rarely seen such a violent storm. I'm inclined to get a room and wait this out."

"It could be a long wait," Collin said. "This is one of those atmospheric rivers. And it's just getting started."

The waitress returned with two plates of food. She handed Collin his meatloaf platter and beamed at Marcel. "Here's your herb-roasted chicken. It's my favorite."

"Thank you, my dear. I'm sure it's delectable."

The two tied into their respective dinners. Neither spoke. Marcel sent several text messages updating the situation while Collin read an eBook on his tablet. Periodically he'd check the position of the white dot on the Google map.

Collin polished off his meatloaf platter and watched Marcel meticulously work his knife and fork to pick the last bits of chicken off the carcass. He snickered. "Wow, I'm impressed. I really am. But that's way too much work. I'd just pick up the damn thing and eat it with my fingers."

Marcel looked at him with a wry smile. "It's called etiquette, my friend, and it's sorely lacking in your generation." He took a sip of coffee and peered out the window. "We should go soon. The rain appears to be tapering off."

"Okay. You want me to drive?"

"You have no choice. We have two cars."

"Oh shit, you're right," Collin replied. He checked his iPad and noticed the flashing dot had moved away from the San Jose airport. "Her plane just took off."

Marcel leaned across the table to see for himself. "I must use the toilet. Perhaps you could ask our waitress for the check. And if you happen to pay, please leave a generous tip."

———

Marcel left the restroom and walked back to the booth. Collin looked up at him. "Are you sure she's flying to Paris?"

"Yes. Why?"

"Because her plane is way out over the Pacific and isn't turning around."

Together they stared at the flashing dot.

"I'm sorry," Collin said, "but she's not going to Paris. Unless the pilot is taking the scenic route."

Marcel stroked his chin. "Interesting."

"I'm telling you; she's flying to Singapore."

chapter seventeen

Rogelio Galvan was bench testing a check valve in Cal Power's maintenance shop on Friday morning when he heard the ringtone. He removed his phone from a back pocket and cursed when he saw the call was not from Sarah.

"Hey, Margaret, what's up?"

"Sorry to bother you, but I was just wondering if you've talked to Sarah recently."

"No, I haven't," he replied with a hint of anger in his voice. "Why?"

"I'm worried about her. Neil sent her home two days ago because she was coming down with a cold. She's been off work since but hasn't called in sick. I've tried to reach her a couple of times, but she's not answering her phone."

"Now that you mention it, she's not answering my calls either," Rogelio said. He debated telling Margaret about their Tuesday evening spat but decided against it. "Did she mention anything to you about an article she's writing?"

"No. Why?"

"Never mind. I'll get back to you."

Rogelio called Sarah and got her voicemail greeting. He walked to Vince Hartman's office and stuck his head through the door. "I have to leave for a couple of hours. Something came up."

"No problem, Ro. Do what you gotta do."

Rogelio hurried to his truck and drove thirty-seven miles to Redwood City. He pulled up in front of Sarah's house and parked behind her Honda Civic.

He ran to the front door, unlocked it, and entered her house. "Sarah, it's me," he called out and went to the bedroom. She wasn't there. He noticed her unmade bed, and his heart raced. She always made the bed. First thing every morning.

"Sarah!"

He went into the kitchen and saw an envelope on the table with his name written on it. He removed a letter from inside the envelope and read her hand-scribed words.

My Dear Rogelio,

 Tears are filling my eyes as I write this. I've made the very painful decision to leave you and start a new life far away from California.

 Meeting you was a godsend. You made me happier than I'd ever been. But when we're not together, my life has no joy. And that's frightening.

I've decided I have to get away—to figure out what's wrong with me, and to try and regain a sense of purpose.

I regret that I didn't have the strength to share my pain with you, but I was raised to be tough and to never reveal weakness.

I will forever hold dear my memories of you. You're truly a wonderful man, and you deserve an equal partner—not someone who uses your love and strength to mask their sadness.

I wish you the very best in your life and can only hope that someday you'll be able to forgive me.

All my love,
Sarah

He collapsed in a chair and read the letter a second time. And a third time.

After the initial shock wore off, he called her and heard a ringtone coming from inside the house. He ran into her bedroom, opened a nightstand drawer, and saw her iPhone.

He stared at its lit-up screen and remembered Vince Hartman's cryptic message: "She wants you to use my office phone and call her. She said it's very important."

Sarah observed the impromptu fashion show of business suits, ao dais, designer jeans, and hijabs inside Paris's Charles de Gaulle Airport as international travelers and

their obedient suitcases paraded by in crisscross directions. Conversations in exotic languages resonated off
the windows of upscale boutiques. On a nearby wall, a
monitor displayed a constantly updating status of flights
to Kyiv, Damascus, Beirut, and other destinations. The
entire world seemed to be at war, but all nations shared
this space in harmony and with common purpose.

Despite her triumphs, she was unable to smile. Twelve
hours and five pain pills after EuropeAir Flight 1532 lifted off the ground in San Jose, her left hand still throbbed,
and her right elbow was tender, courtesy of Jon's face. In
addition, she'd slept very little the past five nights, and her
confinement to a narrow seat with little legroom during
the trans-Atlantic flight only exacerbated her fatigue. She
longed to check into a hotel and crash. But first, there was
work to do.

She walked into a nearby women's restroom and emptied everything in her backpack onto the diaper-changing
table. She inspected each compartment and every inch of
stitching and then checked her running shoes, clothing,
and toiletries. Finding no tracking devices, she repacked
and left. She purchased an untraceable phone, sat down
near a deserted gate, and made her first call.

"NYU School of Medicine."

"Hi, Andrea. This is Dr. Sarah Brenalen. We spoke
yesterday."

"Yes. How could I forget?"

Sarah ignored her sarcasm. "Did you give Paul my
note?"

"No. He's on vacation."

She slumped in her chair. "Are you serious?"

"Yes."

"Do you have any idea where he went?"

Andrea didn't respond.

"I need to know."

"Then why don't you listen to his message? And stop bothering me. Don't call here again."

Sarah cursed and redialed the number. Opting to steer clear of Andrea, she navigated her way to the staff directory and entered the first three letters of Paul's last name.

"Hi, you've reached Paul Johansen. I'm away from my office, enjoying a well-deserved Caribbean vacation. I'll be back on October fifteenth. If this is urgent, please call me on my cell at 212-555-4983." Sarah ended the call and repeated his phone number until she found a pen and wrote it down.

She next called the Cal Power maintenance department and asked Vince Hartman if she could speak with Rogelio.

"He's not here. He left work for a few hours."

"Did you give him my message?"

"I tried, but he said you need to call him."

"I can't. That's why—"

"Ma'am, I don't want to get involved in your personal business. You guys need to work this out yourselves. Okay? Goodbye."

"Goddammit!" Sarah yelled and smacked the phone against her thigh. "Can I catch a break?"

After taking a minute to calm down, she joined the

long line of new arrivals proceeding through Customs. Eighteen minutes later, a uniformed man stamped her passport, and she was officially cleared to enter France.

She changed $1,000 into euros, walked to a tourist information center, and asked an agent if he spoke English.

"Yes, I do. How may I help you?"

"I need a place to stay."

He frowned. "Unfortunately, I only have a few vacancies. And they're very high-end."

"That's okay. I want a nice place."

"Well then, I can offer you a lovely suite at Hôtel L'Impériale. It's in the heart of old Paris. The special rate is 895 euros, with a three-night minimum stay."

Sarah's jaw dropped. Between the two phones, the bottle of wine, the Breezeway, Damien's tip, and her airfare, she'd already spent over a thousand dollars. And Jon had stolen five thousand. This hotel bill could sap the rest of her cash.

"You don't have anything cheaper?"

"No."

Too exhausted to search for alternative lodging, she reluctantly gave in. "Fine. I'll take three nights."

She handed him her passport and scoured the terminal—not exactly sure what she was looking for. Perhaps Marcel or Collin. Or a stranger eyeballing her or walking in her direction. There was nothing that raised suspicion.

The agent completed the reservation and returned her passport. "You are confirmed for three nights. Excuse me for asking, but is this your first visit to Paris?"

"Yes."

"Then allow me to explain. Paris is a relatively safe city, but we have criminals who prey on tourists. So be aware of your surroundings. And keep your valuables secure at all times."

"I will."

"And avoid the Metro. Pickpockets will target you. Taxis are much better."

"Okay."

"So, madam: The fixed rate for a taxi to your hotel is sixty euros. Leave through the door on your right, and you'll see the official taxi queue." He smiled at her. "I wish you a pleasant holiday."

"Thanks."

Sarah walked outside the terminal, and an orange vested airport worker directed her to a cab. A thin Black man was standing next to the open trunk.

"Hôtel L'Impériale," she announced.

Seeing that his passenger was *sans bagage*, the driver closed the trunk, and they both got in.

"*Parlez-vous français?*" he asked as he pulled into traffic.

"Sorry. I only speak English."

"No problem. My name is Daouda Toure. Welcome. Is this your first visit to Paris?"

"Yes."

He got onto a highway, and Sarah looked out the window at unimpressive scenery. She closed her scratchy eyes and was on the verge of sleep when her driver got off the freeway. He came to a stop at a red light, and she regained her focus. He turned onto an eighteenth-century boulevard, and she was instantly mesmerized by the panorama of Gothic and Renaissance architecture.

"Place de la Nation," Daouda said, bearing to the right and driving alongside a circular plaza that featured an illuminated monument. Several avenues converged here, and he casually avoided a collision while relaying the history of this spot. She watched his white teeth and expressive mouth in the rearview mirror and knew he was proud of his city. Or, most likely, his adopted city.

"So, where are you from?" Sarah asked.

"Côte d'Ivoire. In West Africa."

"Your English is quite good."

"Thank you. I speak five languages—French, Baoulé, Senari, English, and Spanish."

"Wow, that's amazing."

"Place de la Bastille," he said, and Sarah gawked at another plaza with magnificent fountains and a grand obelisk rising a couple of hundred feet into the sky.

As impressed as she was by the scenery, her cynical side wondered if these plazas were really on the way to the hotel, or if she was being taken for a ride literally and figuratively.

Daouda pumped the brakes and entered a cobblestone alleyway where pedestrians outnumbered automobiles. The cab maneuvered through foot traffic and rocked on the uneven pavement. Sarah looked out the window at a mix of restaurants, boutiques, and nightclubs just an arm's length away. He stopped at a court-yard.

"Hôtel L'Impériale."

"Great. How much do I owe you?"

"Sixty euros."

She handed Daouda a hundred euro note, thanked him for his informative travelogue, and told him to keep the change.

The concierge welcomed her and opened a massive door crafted from glass and bronze. She walked inside the hotel and passed beneath a crystal chandelier before reaching the reception counter.

"Hi. I believe I have a reservation. My name is Sarah Brenalen."

A man wearing a burgundy suit and strong cologne smiled at her. "Yes, we've been expecting you."

"I'm sorry, but my credit card was stolen. I hope you accept cash."

"We do," he said. "But without a card on file, you'll have to leave a 500-euro deposit and your driver's license."

"Sure."

After receiving the cash and license, he scanned her passport and returned it along with a keycard. "You are confirmed for three nights. Suite 405. Do you have ad-ditional luggage?"

"No. I travel light."

"So I see. Very well. Clément will show you to your suite."

"Thank you."

The gray-uniformed bellboy led Sarah into a tiny elevator. They rode to the fourth floor, and she followed him down the hallway. He stopped at a hardwood door with the number 405 engraved near eye level and slid a keycard into the lock. They entered the suite, and Sarah's eyes bulged. This was something out of *Lifestyles of the Rich and Famous*.

Clément gave her a comprehensive tour of the kitchen, the living room, the bathroom, and the master bedroom. Finally, the *pièce de résistance*. He pulled double doors that opened onto a private balcony and stunning views of the Left Bank. In the distance, the glittering profile of the Eiffel Tower.

Sarah thanked Clément for the tour, pressed some euros into his hand, and locked the door after he left. She took another Tylenol, removed the dressing from her swollen hand, and held it under a stream of cold water at the kitchen sink. After rewrapping the wound, she unpacked her clothes and put the remaining stack of hundred-dollar bills in a safe.

She walked into the bathroom, unbraided her hair, and got undressed. It was decision time: bath or shower. A candlelit bath with Moroccan rose oil in the porcelain tub? Perhaps tomorrow night. She opened the glass door to a quadruple-size shower, pulled a handle, and saw water dispense from the thousand-nozzle "rainforest" feature. After settling on the right temperature, she stepped inside and extended her left hand to keep the bandaged fingers dry.

The bar of soap lathered nicely, and Sarah scrubbed her body with her right hand, determined to wash away any remaining molecules of Jon. She squeezed her eyes shut and stood beneath jets of hot water that prickled her forehead. It was both a glorious facial massage and a symbolic cleansing of the mind that would hopefully dislodge the terrifying images recently burned into her consciousness.

After a twenty-minute shower, she wrapped herself in a Missoni robe and pulled the complimentary bottle of Dom Pérignon from a silver ice bucket. She eschewed the delicate flutes and instead filled a large glass with champagne. Savoring her first sip, she sat down at the computer in the suite's living room.

With one and a half working hands, she accessed the Internet and typed, "Is a person's name stored in a database when their passport is scanned at an airport?"

Amongst the answers was one from a "high-ranking security officer." He wrote, "Your passport is scanned to see if you're on a government's No-Fly list. Names are only scanned—not stored."

She took a few more sips of champagne and typed her next question: "Is there an international database that stores the names of hotel guests?" The answer was no. It would be impossible due to the sheer number of travelers, hotels, and the variety of computers and registration software programs used in the tourist industry.

Encouraged by the answers to her queries, she read the latest news on CNN. When she was out of champagne and interesting stories, she braided her hair and tried to convince herself that everything was going to be okay.

Gravity soon proved victorious over her neck muscles, and her eyelids drooped. She lumbered into the bedroom, removed her robe, and slipped between satin sheets onto the king-size bed. Covered by a sumptuous quilt, she closed her eyes and exhaled a deep breath.

———

The combination of sleep deprivation, champagne, and a comfortable mattress do not guarantee a swift transition into the arms of Morpheus. Sarah learned this lesson as she stared into blackness. Anxieties and fears have a way of asserting themselves after your head hits the pillow.

She envisioned Marcel checking into the suite next door and preparing his gun for duty. And she replayed her gruesome fight with Jon. Was he dead? If so, she'd just murdered a human being—a not insignificant fact that would haunt her for years to come. But if he'd survived, that could mean retribution.

Desperate to sleep, she imagined herself lying on a blanket next to Rogelio on Ka'anapali Beach. The soothing sound of three-foot breakers. Warm sun. Deep breathing. Heart rate slowing.

———

Sarah awoke with a dry mouth. She donned her robe and walked into the kitchen to get a bottle of water. As she opened the refrigerator, a hand grabbed her wrist. She screamed and spun toward her attacker.

"You stabbed me, you bitch," Jon snarled, his shattered face almost unrecognizable. Blood spurted from his neck and trickled down the front of her robe. She kneed him in the groin and punched him twice with her free hand. He released his grip and staggered backward.

Sarah fled Suite 405, ran down three flights of stairs, and out the front door. She raced to the end of the courtyard and came upon an urban forest. She stopped and looked back. Jon was ten meters behind and closing fast. She chose a white stone path and began running through the woods. With each stride, the path narrowed, and the forest encroached. The path soon disappeared, and she found herself racing along a dirt trail—her elbows scraping tree branches, her bare feet leaving clouds of grit in their wake. She ran until the trail ended abruptly at a stream.

Gasping for air, she turned around and saw Marcel and a young boy standing a short distance away. The boy was aiming a rifle at her head. He seemed nervous, and the barrel of his rifle quivered. Marcel attempted to calm the youngster while coaxing him to squeeze the trigger.

Her eyes popped open. Her heart pounded. It was pitch black, and she lay in bed in an unfamiliar room.

———

Margaret Owens received a call from the MEREIN receptionist. "Rogelio Galvan is here to see you."

She wasn't expecting a visit and tried to hide her concern. "Sure. Tell him I'm ready for our meeting."

Rogelio walked into Margaret's office grim-faced. He closed the door behind him and extended Sarah's letter. She took it and started reading.

"*What?* 'I've made the very painful decision to *leave* you.' Is this a joke?"

"No."

Margaret finished reading the letter and looked up at him with bulging eyes. "Oh . . . my . . . god."

She stood, walked around her desk, and they shared a long, silent hug.

Rogelio eventually let go of his grasp and wiped away a tear. "We need to talk."

"Absolutely."

They sat down, and Margaret pulled out a tissue and dabbed her eyes. "I'm stunned. This is crazy. I can't believe she would just take off."

"Me neither."

"Sarah and I talk every day. We confide in each other. She never said anything about being depressed."

"I don't think Sarah *is* depressed. That letter might be bogus," Rogelio said. He went on to describe her odd behavior Tuesday night after he paid her a surprise visit.

"Bottom line: She didn't want to see me. She actually told me to leave. I thought she had another guy in the house."

Margaret flinched. "Oh, come on. You know better than that."

"But what if someone had just broken in? And he threatened to kill us both if she didn't get rid of me. And then, after I left, he made her write that letter. And he kidnapped her."

"Are you serious?"

"If she was leaving town, why didn't she take her car? Or her clothes? Why is there still food in the refrigerator?"

Margaret read the letter again. "But this looks like her handwriting. And I don't see any clues that she was writing under duress."

"Yesterday Sarah called my boss and told him our phones had been hacked. She bought a new one and wanted me to call her using *his* phone. She said it was urgent."

"Did you call her?"

"No. I was still pissed off about Tuesday. But I've called her five times since I read that letter. She's not answering. All I know is . . . nothing makes sense right now. I'm going to the police."

"Why? You can't file a missing-person report."

"I want to know if there have been any recent break-ins in her neighborhood. Or if a registered sex offender lives on her block. Or a Peeping Tom. I just need to talk to someone. Will you come with me?"

———

Rogelio and Margaret left the Redwood City police station after meeting with Detective James Winniford. They were walking to their car when Rogelio saw the sign for Mountain View Pub.

"I could use a drink. How 'bout you?"

They changed course, went into the bar, and sat down at a wooden table.

"I'm glad we talked to him," Rogelio said. "I think you're right. She wasn't kidnapped. And that's good. At least we know her life isn't in danger."

Margaret nodded. "Like he said, it's extremely rare for an adult to be kidnapped. It's usually abuse or depression that causes someone to just up and leave. I know you didn't abuse her, so that leaves depression."

"What can I say? It's hard to accept."

"For you and me both," Margaret said. "She hid her depression very well. A lot of people do. But she wrote that letter. Those are her words."

"I know. I just wish she could have told me. I would have done anything to help her."

Margaret took a moment to consider her response. "Depression isn't an easy thing to talk about. There's a lot of shame associated with it. So, she probably decided her only option was to get away. From you. From me. From MEREIN. From everybody. Just to be alone and work things out."

"I still can't explain why she called my boss and told him our phones had been hacked."

"That *is* weird. But we don't know her state of mind."

A waitress came over to the table, took their order, and walked away. Margaret squeezed Rogelio's hand.

"And speaking of which, how's *your* state of mind?"

He frowned. "Not good. I'm numb right now."

"Me too," she said.

"And I know this is probably wrong, but I'm still pissed off at her."

"I understand. Just remember: Sarah's strong. And resilient. She's going to be okay. And I know she loves you very much. Give her some time. I'm sure she'll call, and you guys will get back together."

Rogelio shook his head. "I don't think so."

chapter eighteen

———

Sarah got out of bed, put on her robe, and walked into the living room. She swung open the doors to her private balcony and was immediately blinded by the sun. It had risen just above the bell tower of a cathedral but had yet to warm the chilly air. She stepped out onto the wrought-iron enclosure, hugged herself to retain body heat, and watched the bustle of activity on the patchwork of cobblestone streets below.

She returned to her bedroom, got dressed, and went downstairs to the hotel restaurant. After eating breakfast—croissant with jam, quiche Lorraine, and a grande cappuccino—she walked to the lobby and spotted the concierge. "Hi, I need to go to the U.S. Embassy."

"I'm sorry, but it's closed," he said. "It's open Monday through Friday."

"Oh, okay. Thank you."

She jogged up to the fourth floor, entered her suite,

and sat down at the computer. She did a search for "U.S. Embassy in Paris," opened the home page, and saw the word "Closed."

She called the phone number and heard a recorded message: "You have reached the embassy of the United States of America. Our business hours are from 9 a.m. to 5 p.m. Monday through Friday. Please call back during those times. *Vous êtes arrivé à l'Ambassade des États-Unis d'Amérique. Les heures. . . .*"

She next tried the FBI, knowing it was early Saturday morning in Washington, DC. A recording announced their business hours and instructed the caller to dial 911 if this was an emergency.

Undeterred, she typed "U.S. Homeland Security" and called their twenty-four-hour hotline. A man answered, and she was taken aback. "Oh, my god. You're not a recording."

"Do you have a security threat to report?"

"Yes."

"Okay," he said. "First of all, please know that everything you say is being recorded."

"That's fine."

"Then go ahead."

She decided to keep her initial statement brief. In ten seconds, she gave her name and occupation and explained that terrorists had gotten a sample of her brain-destroying drug and were going to reproduce it and carry out an attack.

"An attack against whom?" he asked.

"I don't know."

"I understand. And I appreciate your call. But this is an after-hours hotline for reporting an imminent attack against the United States."

"Yes, but—"

"I suggest you call back on Monday. If your story is credible, we'll assign you a case number and get on it."

"Okay, but I'm afraid—"

"Thank you for your help in keeping America safe. Goodbye."

Sarah threw down her phone. "And thank *you* for blowing me off," she said before acknowledging that he was right. His job was to prevent an *imminent* attack—the nutcase driving an explosives-laden truck to the Capital or a suicide bomber boarding an airplane. A T-3 attack, on the other hand, was *not* imminent. It was unlikely they'd even produced an ingestible sample of her drug.

She leaned back in her chair, rubbed her eyes, and realized there was no need to panic. She could wait until Monday morning. But instead of calling Homeland Security and being assigned a case number, she'd go to the U.S. Embassy.

With a new plan in place, she focused on her left hand, which was now begging for help. She peeled off the surgical tape, unwrapped several layers of gauze, and was shocked to see a portobello mushroom-like growth at the base of the baby finger. She left her suite, ran down three flights of stairs, and approached the concierge.

"Hi. I need to get to a hospital."

"Please come with me," he said and escorted her to a waiting taxi.

———

After sitting for twelve minutes in the Hôpital de Paris waiting room, Dr. Arjun Patel examined her left hand and ordered an x-ray. It confirmed her suspicion—a broken finger.

"This might sting a bit," the doctor warned before giving her a shot of lidocaine. He was right. But she was glad her hand was numb as she watched him drain putrid fluid from the base of the finger and cleanse the wound. After applying a yellow ointment that stained her skin, he splinted the finger and wrapped it with white gauze.

"I think it will heal on its own, but you may want to see a doctor when you get home," he said. "In the meantime, don't remove this dressing. And keep it dry."

Sarah thanked Dr. Patel for his decorum and competence and left the treatment room. She stopped by the pharmacy to pick up her prescription pain pills and purchased five syringes.

On her way back to the hotel, she saw throngs of people enjoying the city on this gorgeous day and got inspired.

She returned to her suite, pulled *Walking Paris* off a bookshelf, and considered five of its itineraries. She chose the most ambitious one—a seven-mile loop that included Notre Dame, Hôtel de Ville, the Louvre, Tuileries Garden, the Arc de Triomphe, and the Eiffel Tower. Wishing to stay hydrated, she grabbed a bottle of water from the refrigerator. Wishing to stay alive, she filled one of her newly purchased syringes with Entoryl-XT and slid it into a side pocket of her cargo pants. Just in case.

Sarah navigated her way from Hôtel L'Impériale to Île de la Cité and to the first destination on her itinerary: Notre Dame Cathedral. After taking two photos of its famous towers, she crossed a bridge to the Marais district on the right bank of the Seine and walked alongside historic Hôtel de Ville.

At Rue de Rivoli, she headed west and was captivated by the nineteenth-century buildings that lined both sides of the street. Restaurants and boutiques dominated the ground floors, while apartments occupied the upper four or five stories. She focused on one apartment—its balcony enclosed by an intricate, wrought-iron railing—and imagined sharing it with Rogelio. Was that a crazy idea?

After walking past the massive Louvre complex, she stepped inside a delicatessen and joined a dozen lunchtime customers eyeing display cases filled with meat, cheese, salads, and desserts. She purchased a take-out lunch, continued on, and soon reached Tuileries Garden.

The park was teeming with tourists and Parisians of all generations on this warm October afternoon. She eventually claimed an unoccupied bench, removed a ham-and-brie-stuffed baguette from a paper bag, took a bite, and reveled in the myriad sights and sounds. Families and lovers strolled the sidewalks. Picnickers and sunbathers dotted the expansive lawn. Two old women scattered bits of bread for the pigeons. Children laughed as they ran through the waterspouts of a fountain. A disheveled man bellowed a soulful rendition of *Autumn Leaves* on his saxophone.

She ate slowly, savoring the moment and each bite of her stuffed baguette. When there was nothing left but crumbs, she finished off the bottle of water and resumed her walking tour. At the north end of Tuileries Garden, she saw the Arc de Triomphe in the distance. Unfortunately, it was a rather long distance. With a full stomach and the effects of jet lag weighing her down, she decided to turn around. It was time to head back to her suite and take a well-deserved nap.

Sarah retraced her steps through Tuileries Garden and down Rue de Rivoli—stopping periodically to admire the fashions in upscale stores—before eventually coming upon an unrecognizable open-air market. A brass plaque identified the spot as Place Baudoyer. She grudgingly looked at a map in *Walking Paris* and realized she'd overshot her route back to the hotel. After deciding on a new route, she walked through Place Baudoyer and saw three police cars and four uniformed officers in front of a building. What at first appeared to be a crime scene was, in fact, the entrance to a police station. Just thirty feet away. And the two front doors were open. It occurred to her that she could walk inside and sound the T-3 alarm.

As she approached the station, one of the officers hopped on a bicycle and pedaled away. Two others got into a car and drove off. The fourth officer remained outside. He eyed her and spoke kind words in French.

Was he hitting on her? Inviting her to come in? It was decision time. She hesitated, shook her head, and kept walking.

In fits and starts, Sarah found her way back to Hôtel L'Impériale. She rode the elevator to the fourth floor and saw a woman standing in front of an adjacent suite. They exchanged smiles. She pulled out her keycard, thought for a moment, and then turned to face the woman.

"Excuse me. Do you speak English?"

"A little bit, yes," the woman said.

"Great. I was just wondering if it's safe for me to walk around this area alone at night."

"Well," the woman replied, "I would say the Latin Quarter is safe. But be careful because of pickpockets. They try to steal from tourists."

"So I've been told. Thanks for the heads-up."

She slid her keycard into the slot, entered Suite 405, and saw a vase of white roses on the kitchen countertop. Propped up against the vase was an envelope that read "Courtoisie de Hôtel L'Impériale" in embossed calligraphy. She opened the envelope and pulled out a complimentary ticket to the Orsay Museum. "Wow," she whispered to herself, "this place is awesome."

She grabbed a bottle of sparkling water from the refrigerator, guzzled it down with two prescription pain pills, did a round of stretching, and made her way into the bedroom.

―――

Collin Smith retrieved his phone after hearing the first two measures of Kraftwerk's *Computer Love*. "Hey, old man. I hope you had a pleasant drive back. I almost got blown off the road."

"I offer you no sympathy," Marcel said. "If memory serves me, I suggested we wait out the storm."

"Yeah, I suppose you did. Lesson learned. So, what's up?"

"Two things. First, I sent the syringe to our lab people. They're going to analyze it and tell me what Sarah injected herself with. Second, I wanted you to know that Jon is no longer with us."

"What?" Collin blurted out. "He died?"

"No. He's no longer *working* with us."

"Aah. That would be different. You see how adding just one word to that sentence changes everything?"

"Yes," Marcel replied. "Thank you very much for the English grammar lesson."

"Any time. So, is he still recovering from the Sarah beat-down?"

"Yes. But I sacked him because he's incompetent. He let her escape. That was inexcusable. Now we have to go to Paris and track her down."

"Paris? The GPS shows her in Singapore."

"And two days ago, the GPS showed her at home when she was actually at a bank withdrawing two million dollars."

"You're right," Collin said. "I'd forgotten about that. So, you're sure she's in Paris?"

"I sent my colleague her photo. He went to Charles de Gaulle Airport, saw her get off a plane, and followed her to a hotel."

"Damn. And here I was all set to fly to Singapore."

"May I repeat: underestimate her at your peril."

Paul Johansen sat in a bamboo chair beneath a large umbrella that shaded him from the morning sun. He sipped coffee and read the news on his phone as reggae music played through the resort's sound system.

"Excuse me," came a woman's voice with a lovely accent. "Do you think I could borrow your phone?"

Paul looked up at the bikini-clad woman. Thirty-ish. Medium height. Tanned body. Shoulder-length, blonde hair. Pretty face. "You want to use my phone?"

"I forgot to charge mine last night, and I have an important call to make."

He gave her a skeptical eye. His guidebook warned that criminals take advantage of tourists who let down their guard while enjoying a Caribbean vacation.

"Here," she said, twisting a jewel-encrusted ring off her finger and placing it in front of him on the small table. "It has a one-carat diamond. You can keep it as collateral."

Paul grimaced. "That's not necessary."

"I'm going through a divorce, so I won't be wearing it much longer anyway."

Feeling even lower, he closed the *New York Times* app and extended his phone to her. "I'm sorry. It's just that I don't know you, and—"

"It's okay. I hope you don't mind, but this is a private matter. I'm staying over there," she said, pointing to a door with the number 6 on it.

"No problem."

"I'll be back in five minutes."

The woman walked away with Paul's phone, entered her room, and locked the door behind her. She scrolled through his phone log and all of his text messages. She then picked up her phone and called Marcel. "I don't see any communication between Paul and Sarah."

"Good."

"So, when will the package arrive?"

"Hopefully soon. The lab is experiencing some difficulty producing an ingestible T-3."

"Keep me posted."

Switching back to Paul's phone, she called an insurance office in Paris and asked an agent several questions before hanging up. That was all she needed—proof of an international call. She left her room, walked back to Paul's table, and handed him his phone.

"Thank you so much," she said as she picked up her wedding ring and slid it over her finger.

"Did you make your call?" he asked.

"Yes. Unfortunately, he's being a real asshole."

"I'm sorry to hear that."

The woman smiled. "I don't care. The divorce should be final in a week, and I'll be free to start a new life."

———

Sarah awoke after a few hours of sleep and stared at the ceiling. She longed for Rogelio. His smile. His voice. His jokes. His strong arms holding her tight against his naked body in bed. His soft kisses. His unshaven face rubbing against hers.

It was now Saturday morning in California. They should be enjoying breakfast together and planning a day of house hunting. At least that was the plan before their Tuesday evening fight.

No doubt he was still furious—and growing increasingly agitated—as he waited for her to apologize and explain why she'd been so cold to him.

Was he still calling? Had he come over Friday evening as planned? If so, had Marcel left the note behind for him to read? Her heart ached at the thought. She suppressed tears and reassured herself that Rogelio would soon learn the truth. Hopefully, he'd forgive her.

She took a shower with her newly treated hand protected by a plastic bag and then put on her finest. She posed in front of the full-length bedroom mirror and acknowledged that her pants and top wouldn't find a home in any of the stores on Rue de Rivoli. So be it.

She stepped out onto her private balcony to check the weather. A fine mist saturated the evening air. The moisture was more palpable than fog but not substantive enough to be called rain. She decided not to take the hotel-issue umbrella, but—having been warned about thieves—put her wallet, phone, and syringe of Entoryl-XT into her zippered pants pockets.

Sarah left Hôtel L'Impériale and stepped into an Impressionist painting. Boutiques, galleries, and cafes glowed in the mist. Streets and sidewalks glistened. She walked two blocks in no particular direction, entered an enticing restaurant, and ordered duck confit à l'orange and a *pichet* of red wine.

Eighty minutes later, while savoring the last bite of crêpes amandine and sipping espresso, she thought about Paul and wondered where in the Caribbean he was vacationing. The Cayman Islands? Aruba? Cozumel? She doubted it. Paul never struck her as being much of a beach resort kind of guy. If he'd gone to an island, it would be to stimulate his brain. She imagined him lying on a rocky, wind-swept beach in the Galapagos, studying the mating rituals of iguanas, and smiled.

Suddenly her face grew taut. What if Paul *wasn't* on vacation? What were the odds he'd go to the Caribbean *this week*?

She now imagined Marcel spreading the handles of his Neiman Marcus shopping bag and asking Paul to look inside. The possibility that he'd been kidnapped and was being forced to help them produce an ingestible T-3 sent a chill through her body. She desperately wanted to call him but feared putting his life in danger.

Her waiter came by and picked up the check and a one hundred euro note from the table. While awaiting her change, she came up with an idea: She'd call him—just to hear his voice and know he was okay. But, to play it safe, she'd make the call far away from Hôtel L'Impériale. And disguise her voice.

Sarah left the restaurant and walked to a waiting taxi. She was about to get in but hesitated when she saw the entrance to the Saint-Michel Metro station. This unexpected choice between modes of transportation produced a moment of indecision.

At Charles de Gaulle Airport, the well-intentioned

tourist information agent had warned her against using the Metro. While she appreciated his concern, a part of her resented being tagged a gullible American. She was streetwise and had ridden subways in the Bay Area, New York City, and Chicago without incident.

Don't be a wimp.

Sarah proceeded with confidence to the Metro station, skipped down two flights of stairs, and purchased a ticket. She descended more stairs and joined several others on the platform. According to an overhead monitor, the next train would arrive in one minute. The train after that in four minutes. She observed the ever-increasing number of commuters gathering around her and decided it was a good thing trains came in quick succession.

As promised, a train swooshed into the station within a minute. It was almost filled to capacity. The doors opened, and a few passengers got off. Sarah made her way inside, grabbed hold of a pole, and fought to maintain her grip as people squeezed in behind her. When the accumulated mass could compress no further, the doors closed, and the train departed. She felt bodies pressing against her and feared someone might be trying to steal her phone or wallet. Letting go of the pole, she clutched her pockets and scrutinized the others sharing this tight space.

The train sped through the tunnel and soon rolled into the next station. The doors opened, people spilled out, and she could breathe easily again. A smaller number of commuters came aboard, the doors closed, and the train accelerated toward its next destination.

Over time she noticed a pattern: with each stop, the car became less crowded, and the percentage of darker-skinned passengers increased. While debating how long to ride the train, she studied the Line 4 Metro map above the door and saw a stop called Château Rouge.

"Château Rouge," she purred with a French accent. It sounded like an expensive bottle of wine.

The train pulled into the Château Rouge station, and Sarah got off. She walked up the stairs behind four Black women wrapped in tie-dye prints and matching headscarves. At street level, she discovered a Paris far removed from the Latin Quarter. The Paris not captured on postcards or frequented by tourists. The faces and clothing of passersby suggested a neighborhood of immigrants—or more precisely, West African immigrants. The neighborhood her taxi driver Daouda Toure perhaps came home to after his shift.

She headed down a busy street lined with shops and cafes—all doing a brisk business on this Saturday night—and listened to animated conversations in languages other than French. She turned onto a quiet side street, pulled out her phone, and called Paul. He answered after one ring. "Hello?"

"Jean-Claude?" she asked with a French accent.

"Who?"

"Ehh . . . Jean-Claude?"

He laughed. "Sorry, you have the wrong number. But feel free to call any time. I love your voice."

"Sank you. Goodbye for now," Sarah said and put her phone away.

Hearing just a few words from Paul was enough to induce a smile. He was alive. And, far from sounding like a kidnap victim, his voice suggested he was indeed enjoying a Caribbean vacation.

The call also assuaged any fears she had about Rogelio. Marcel hadn't killed Paul, so why would he target someone who knew nothing at all about T-3?

Breathing a tremendous sigh of relief, she walked back to the Château Rouge Metro station and skipped down the stairs.

———

Sarah entered her suite and noticed the complimentary ticket to the Orsay Museum on the kitchen counter. An idea popped into her head. Her next-door neighbor had likely received one as well. Why not go there together?

She rang the front desk and asked for the phone number for Suite 404.

"It's four, zero, four. The same number as the suite."

"Wow, what a coincidence," Sarah said while chastising herself for not figuring that out on her own.

"No, the phone numbers and suite numbers are always the same."

"Got it. *Thank you.*"

She hung up and dialed 404. There was no answer.

chapter nineteen

———

Sarah left the Orsay Museum and took a moment to appreciate her visit. For more than two hours, she'd strolled from room to room and from masterpiece to masterpiece with a charming and insightful guide at her side. She reflected and decided it would be hard to beat the Orsay. Sure, the Louvre was bigger and more prominent. And it had the Mona Lisa, for which people would wait an hour just to capture in a selfie. But the Orsay was a treasure trove. If not for fatigue and a grumbling stomach, she would have stayed all day.

She opened her *Walking Paris* guidebook, read the section on dining, and decided to grab lunch at Le Poulpry. The restaurant had earned a rave review and was only a block away. She reached it in two minutes, and a *portier* greeted her and opened the door. She stepped inside, inhaled the beguiling aroma of basil and roasted garlic, and scanned the crowded dining room for an empty seat. A Maître d' noticed her and held up one finger. She nodded, and the tuxedo-clad gentleman led her over to a table.

———

The young woman, wearing a teal bikini and black sunglasses, was reclining in a chair next to the swimming pool and reading a magazine. Occasionally she diverted her eyes to Paul Johansen's suite.

It was 9:37 a.m., and he had yet to make an appearance. A housekeeper pushing a cart stopped in front of his door and knocked. Paul opened the door and stepped outside into the morning sun. He wore a New York Yankees T-shirt, blue shorts, and flip-flops. After exchanging a few words with the cleaning woman, he ambled fifty feet to the restaurant and ordered breakfast.

———

The woman in the teal bikini followed Paul after he left the restaurant. He walked a path to the far edge of Accra Beach and then continued twenty yards across golden sand to the shoreline. He looked out onto turquoise water as gentle waves splashed over his feet.

A musical jingle rang out, taking the woman's eyes away from Paul. She pulled a phone from inside her tote bag, noticed the number, and answered the call.

"Hey, Marcel. What's happening?"

"Your package will arrive today. Be in your room between fifteen and nineteen hundred hours."

"Okay."

"Are you ready?"

"Not yet, but I'm close."

"George wants this done tonight."

"I know."

She ended the call and followed Paul as he walked the shoreline. He reached the western tip of Accra Beach and turned around. She drew within a few feet of him and smiled, as if recognizing an old friend. "Hey," she said, "didn't I borrow your phone yesterday?"

Paul stopped and studied her face. "Yes, you did. Do you need to use it again?"

"No, thank god. The less I talk to my ex, the better." She walked up to him and offered an alluring gaze. "I don't mean to be nosy, but are you staying here alone?"

"Yes. Why?"

"I was just wondering if you'd like some company tonight."

Paul's eyes lit up, and she raised her hands in a defensive posture. "For the record, I'm not hitting on you, okay? But I've been here for five days, and I'm tired of talking to myself."

"Sure. I understand," he said.

"I'd invite you over, but my room is tiny. And I noticed you have one of those deluxe suites."

"I do. And yes, you're welcome to come over."

She smiled. "Thanks. Maybe we could watch a movie. Have a couple of drinks. You know, just hang out."

"Absolutely," Paul said. "I have a big-screen TV and a bunch of DVDs."

"Great. By the way, I'm Erika."

"And I'm Paul," he said as they shook hands.

"Do you like Manhattans?" she asked.

"I do. Why?"

"I make a killer Manhattan. So how about this: you pick the movie, and I'll provide the libations."

"Sounds like a plan."

"Then I'll see you tonight. Around seven-ish?"

"Seven it is," he replied. "And thanks for taking the initiative."

They parted ways, and Paul contemplated what type of movie would be appropriate for the evening. And he wondered if perhaps—Erika's words to the contrary—a little romance could make its way onto the evening's agenda.

———

Sarah walked along the Seine back to Hôtel L'Impériale, still savoring her orgasmic, five-star lunch at Le Poulpry. She entered the lobby and heard someone call out her name. She turned and made eye contact with her next-door neighbor in Suite 404. The woman smiled and approached her.

"Did you avoid the pickpockets last night?"

Sarah laughed. "Yes, I did."

"Good. Remember to keep your eyes always alert."

"I will. Thanks."

Sarah jogged up three flights of stairs, entered her suite, and saw a gift basket on the kitchen counter. It contained a bottle of wine, crackers, a wedge of Brie, an energy drink, and chocolate truffles. Another classy touch from this magnificent hotel.

She noticed a blinking red light on her hotel phone, picked up the receiver, and listened to a recorded message: "Thank you for patronizing Hôtel L'Impériale. We hope you have enjoyed your stay. Please check out of your suite before eleven o'clock tomorrow morning. We will happily assist you with any luggage. We wish you fond travels and look forward to your next visit."

Sarah gasped and dropped the receiver.

How does she know my name?

She replayed her initial encounter with the woman. They'd spoken briefly about avoiding pickpockets. That was it. They hadn't introduced themselves. Neither had mentioned her name.

"No, no, no," she moaned, suppressing a scream. "It can't be. How did they find me? *How the fuck . . . ?*"

She grabbed her backpack and began stuffing her belongings inside: clothes from the dresser and closet, toiletries from the bathroom, and the stack of bills from the safe. After taking a quick look around to make sure she'd left nothing behind, she flung the backpack over a shoulder and ran to the door. She opened it and recoiled when she saw her next-door neighbor standing there.

"Oh, hi. I just want to ask—"

Sarah's punch broke the woman's nose and sent her hurtling backward. Her ear-piercing screech stopped when she slammed against the wall and collapsed to the floor.

Sarah ran to the end of the hallway and flew down the stairs. Rounding the third-floor landing, she heard the woman cry out for help. At the second floor, she detected the sound of running feet, and a voice: "Sarah hit me! She's getting away!"

Sarah burst out the front door.

The police station. Where was it? Think, goddammit, think!

She chose left and raced along the pedestrian walkway, doing her best to pass the slower-moving masses while avoiding oncoming foot traffic. At the first intersection, she looked back and saw a man running toward her.

She cursed and bolted down a side street. At the next intersection, she went left. Then right. Then left again. The advantage was hers. She was lithe, fast, and running for her life on a zigzag route through an eighteenth-century maze. Not an ideal place for even a seasoned professional to tail someone.

At the fifth or sixth intersection, she ducked inside a gift shop to catch her breath. While cautiously optimistic she'd ditched the bastard, she'd also lost her bearings. Finding her way out of the Latin Quarter without crossing paths just taken and inadvertently bumping into her potential killer would be tricky. She poked her head outside the gift shop, looked in both directions, and sprinted toward a busy street.

Sarah emerged from the maze at Rue Saint-Jacques and saw the imposing towers of Notre Dame. Her compass. She jogged to hectic Quai de Montebello on the left bank of the Seine and turned around. To her shock, the man was closing in on her.

She jumped into the street and dodged three lanes of honking cars before reaching the other side of Quai de Montebello. Another quick burst took her across Petit

Pont to Île de la Cité. She raced past vendors and street performers and fought her way through tour groups before reaching Notre Dame and gaining the confidence to look back. The man was still on her tail.

Beseeching her body on, she maintained a grueling pace through Île de la Cité, over a bridge to Île Saint-Louis, and down a busy street lined with outdoor cafes. After crossing another bridge to the Right Bank, she ran up an alleyway to a medieval church—one she recognized from her walking tour—and knew Place Baudoyer was nearby. She made it to the end of the block and shrieked when she saw her destination. On the verge of collapse, she staggered across Rue François Miron, through the open doors of the police station, and came to a halt against a long counter.

"Help me!" she pleaded to a bespectacled gentleman standing on the other side of the counter. "There's a guy out there," she managed before gasping for air, "and he—"

"*Je suis désolé. Je ne parle—*"

"I have no idea what you're saying!" Sarah ran to the front door and peeked outside.

"May I help you?" She spun around and saw a middle-aged man wearing a three-piece suit.

"Is this a police station?"

"Yes. I'm Inspector René Vallon. What can I do for you?"

"Some guy just chased me down the street," she said, gesturing out the door. "He was going to kill me."

The inspector's eyes grew, and he barked several words in French. A blue-uniformed policeman rushed into the room, and the two of them came over to her. "Point him out to us," the inspector exhorted.

"No. I just need to call the U.S. ambassador."

"I'm afraid the ambassador can't help you. This is a police matter."

"Can you take me to a private office?"

"But what about the man who tried to kill you?"

Sarah shook her head. "This is much bigger than him."

"Then I'm confused. You said—"

"*Please!* I need to call the ambassador *now*. This is an emergency."

His expression soured. "All right. Come this way."

Sarah followed the men down a hallway and into an office. The inspector closed the door behind them and pointed to two chairs facing his cluttered desk. "Please sit down."

"Thank you," she said and took a seat. The officer sat beside her. The inspector eased into the chair behind his desk and cleared his throat. "I'm sorry, I didn't get your name."

"Sarah Brenalen," she replied as her respiration and heart rate began to ease.

"May I see some identification?"

She pulled out her passport and handed it to him.

He opened it and slowly flipped through the pages. Her right heel started tapping the floor.

"So, what brings you to Paris?"

"Is this necessary? I just want to call the ambassador."

"Fine." He gave Sarah back her passport, retrieved a pair of reading glasses from a desk drawer, and faced his computer. His fingers made clicking sounds as he typed on the keyboard. He turned to Sarah and peered over the top of his designer frames. "You want the *U.S.* ambassador?"

"Yes."

He turned back to his computer monitor. *Clickity clickity click. Clickity click. Tap tap. Click.* He picked up the receiver to his desk phone and dialed several numbers. "His name is Otto Samuels," he said, handing her the receiver.

Sarah heard several dial tones followed by his voice-mail greeting. She left a message imploring him to call her and then gave the receiver back. "That was his office phone."

"Oh," the inspector replied, making no effort to conceal his disinterest in her predicament.

"I need to talk to him."

"And I need to get back to work."

"You don't understand. My life is in danger. They're waiting for me to leave."

"Who?"

"The people trying to kill me."

"Now there's *more* than one person? Just how many people are trying to kill you?"

"Bear with me for a minute," Sarah appealed. "I'm a neuropharmacologist. I work at a research laboratory called MEREIN. A while back, I accidentally discovered a drug that destroys the brain. These people forced me to give them a sample. Now they're trying to reproduce it so they can carry out a terrorist attack. And they want me dead because I'm the only one who can stop them."

The inspector blinked but didn't respond. He didn't have to. His weary expression said it all. She knew he was going to boot her out the door.

"You don't believe me, do you?" Sarah said. "Look up MEREIN on your computer. You'll see that I work there." His phone rang.

"Excuse me," he said and answered the call.

Sarah pulled out her phone and did a search for the name "Otto Samuels." She selected a website titled "U.S. Embassy & Consulates in France" and scrolled through its "Meet Otto Samuels" and "Emergency Services" pages on the off chance his personal phone number was listed. It wasn't.

The inspector ended his call, and Sarah leaned forward to regain his attention. "You have to help me get in touch with Mr. Samuels."

"I just did. You left a message on his phone. Now it's time for you to go."

"No. That guy is still out there. He's waiting for me to leave."

"I asked you to point him out to us. But you refused. However, if you're still worried, I can have one of my men accompany you to a taxi."

"I can't leave here until I reach the ambassador. Or the FBI. Or somebody who can help me."

He looked at the officer sitting beside her and said something to him in French. The man nodded, and she could only assume they were plotting the best way to physically remove her from the premises.

"Wait a minute. Do you have jail cells here?"

"Yes. Why?"

"Let me stay in one of them."

"No. This is not a hotel," he said, and then relayed something to the officer. His quip must have been funny because the young man burst into laughter.

"Why can't I stay in one of your jails?"

"Because you haven't been arrested."

"Don't you have some kind of protective custody?"

"Yes. But you haven't provided me any evidence that you require it."

"I only need to stay here a couple of hours. Maybe one night."

"That would be false imprisonment."

"But I *want* to stay here."

"Then you must commit a crime that warrants arrest and detention."

The policeman kept snickering, obviously tickled by something the inspector had said to him. They didn't believe her. Nor respect her. In their minds, she was just a crazy woman.

"Anything else?"

She forced herself to remain civil. "Yes. One last question: is assaulting a police officer a crime in France?"

"Of course."

"Good."

Sarah stood and looked down at the cop. "Excuse me. You think this is funny?" She lunged at him and locked her hands around his neck. His chair flipped over sideways, and they both went crashing to the floor.

"Hey!" the inspector yelled and jumped to his feet. "Stop!"

Sarah squeezed the officer's neck as they wrestled on the floor. He punched her in the face and tried to pry away her fingers. The inspector rushed over and grabbed her shoulders. The door burst open, and two more men joined the fray. Sarah released her grip of the man's neck and was pulled upright by one of the arriving cops. He pinned her arms behind her back and yelled something in French.

The injured policeman got to his feet and was immediately restrained by one of his colleagues as he spat a nonstop flow of vitriol at Sarah.

The inspector came face to face with her. "You just attacked him! For no reason! You're out of your mind! And you're under arrest for assaulting a police officer!"

Sarah fought for air and glared back at him. "Thank you!"

chapter twenty

Collin Smith stood beneath the awning of a jewelry store in Place Baudoyer. His eyes were so fixated on the police station that he didn't notice his partner walking up from behind.

"What's happening?" Marcel asked.

He snapped his head around. "Nothing. She's still inside."

"Unbelievable. We were so close. And now we're back to square one."

"Worse. She's in a goddamn police station."

"Why do you suppose she ran?" Marcel asked.

Collin shrugged. "I don't know."

"I want you to put trackers on both of those police cars. In case they drive her away."

"Okay. And if they *don't* drive her away?"

"We'll have to come up with a plan to get inside."

"Are you kidding?"

"No, not at all."

But . . . that's a police station."

Marcel smiled. "Don't worry. I have an idea."

During a brief arraignment, the inspector confiscated all of Sarah's belongings and informed her that, according to French law, she had the right to an attorney and the right to make a phone call.

"Do you want me to get you a lawyer?" he asked.

"Yes. And if it's okay, I'd like to wait until tomorrow morning to make my call."

"That's fine. Now come with me."

He led her down a flight of stairs and over to a jail cell. She entered, and he locked its steel door behind her. She looked up at him between the bars. "I'm sorry, I forgot your name."

"It's René."

"That's right. René. I want to apologize for attacking your officer."

He turned and walked away.

Sarah took a seat on the lower bunk bed and elevated her bandaged hand. Her finger throbbed, and she feared that her altercation with the police officers had inflicted new damage.

She punched the mattress with her right fist. "How did they find me?"

The man who'd just chased her looked a lot like Collin. Could he have followed her to Paris? It was doubtful he had enough time to buy a ticket and board her flight. Besides, she would have spotted him in the security line.

Was she wearing another transmitter? No. It was impossible. She'd conducted an exhaustive search of her belongings at the airport and found nothing. And the one she discovered in San Jose would lead them to Singapore, not Paris.

"How *the hell* did they find me?"

Craving a cigarette, she surveyed her tight quarters. In addition to the bed, her eight-by-fourteen-foot cell contained a semi-private toilet and a sink with one faucet. The only lighting came from fluorescent fixtures in the hallway. Along with the white cinder block walls and white steel bars, everything seemed rather cold.

She stood up, walked to her cell door, and noticed that the women's portion of the jail had four cells. The other three were empty. Parisian women were apparently law-abiding citizens.

She heard a noise and saw a policeman and a haggard waif with intense eyes approaching. They stopped in front of her cell. The policeman unlocked her door, and the woman slinked past her and sat on the lower bunk.

"What are you doing?" Sarah demanded. The officer ignored her question and clanged the door shut.

"Hey! Get her out of here!"

He shrugged and walked away.

Sarah whipped around and confronted her new cellmate. "You come near me, and I will *fucking* kill you. Do you understand?" The woman cowered and said a few words in French.

She banged on the steel bars with the palm of her

right hand. "René! Get down here!" She took a step back and kicked the door, producing a loud boom that reverberated for several seconds.

The cellblock door crashed open, and the inspector raced over to her. "What's wrong?"

"I want this woman out of my cell."

"What did she do?"

"Nothing. But I—"

"She did *nothing*? It sounded like you were being murdered."

"I don't trust her."

"Her name is Lisette. I've known her for years."

Sarah was silent for a few seconds before continuing in a more rational tone of voice. "I'm not trying to be difficult, but I don't trust anyone right now. And there are three other cells, so I don't understand why you put her in here with me."

"Lisette's a petty criminal and a prostitute," he said. "Last year, a policeman raped her while she was in jail. Even though it was an isolated incident, she feels safer sharing a cell with another woman."

"I'm sorry that happened. But I still don't want her in here with me."

Lisette pointed at Sarah and pleaded with René. He raised his hands in a reassuring motion.

"Now that you have sufficiently scared her, she also wants to be moved. Can you please get out of the way?"

Sarah stepped to the side, and René opened the cell door. Lisette walked a wide arc around Sarah and entered the facing cell.

"Did you find me a lawyer?"

"I was trying. But then you interrupted me with your outburst." He looked at his watch. "It's almost nineteen hundred hours. Not a good time to find you counsel. Don't disturb me again."

"I won't."

René stormed off. Sarah saw Lisette looking at her and offered an apologetic smile. "Please forgive me. I am so sorry."

———

The cellblock door opened, and Sarah rose from the lower bunk bed. She listened to the click of dress shoes on the cement floor and saw René.

"I found you a lawyer who speaks English."

"You did?"

"Yes. He'll be here in a few minutes. I can't guarantee you he's any good."

"That's okay. Thank you."

"And I need to know if you're a vegetarian."

"No. Why?"

"Because dinner will be served shortly."

"I don't want dinner. Just my lawyer."

"Fine," he said. "Anyway, I'm going home soon."

"You can't stay?"

"No."

"Then can you do me a favor? Before you leave, can you tell whoever's in charge not to allow any visitors down here?"

"No one—with the exception of your lawyer—will be granted access."

"Good. And your guys need to be prepared for an attack."

"I'll pass along your concern."

Sarah snorted and shook her head.

"What?"

"You think I'm crazy, don't you? You think I'm making all this up."

René chose his words carefully. "I'm sure you believe your life is in danger."

She shot him a laser stare. "My life *is* in danger. I'm the only one who can stop them."

He smirked.

"Dammit! This isn't a joke. They have a drug so deadly, a few parts per *billion* could potentially destroy a human brain. What if they inject it into the bottled water going to a school? Or to a session of Congress? Or worse. Imagine them dumping ten gallons of it into a city's treated water supply."

He stole a look at his watch. "Interesting."

"A drop of water from an ice cube or the residual amount you get from brushing your teeth would be enough to render you comatose."

"Aah, but you're forgetting one thing," René noted. "Drinking water is chemically treated."

"So what? You can easily coat a drug so that it's protected from low concentrations of chlorine, ammonia, or ozone. Yet, once swallowed, that same coating will be broken down by stomach acid. The drug would be released as it enters the intestine."

René scratched the side of his face. "Well, I'm not a

chemist or a physician, so I can't dispute what you just said. However, I find it odd that in the hundreds of intelligence reports I've read from around the world regarding terrorist plots, not one has involved poisoning a city's drinking water."

"That's because none of your experts knows about it. So, while everyone is on guard against cyber-attacks and airplane hijackers, treated water supplies are vulnerable. Hit one of them, and you're looking at something worse than 9/11."

"Oh, come on. You really believe that?"

"Yes," Sarah shot back. "Three thousand people were killed on September 11th. It was horrible. But if T-3 is infused into a city's treated water supply, *ten* thousand people might ingest it. Imagine a city with ten thousand brain-dead people."

René laughed. "That sounds like Paris."

"It's not funny. You suddenly have all these people who'll never move or speak again—who must be cared for twenty-four hours a day. Think of the medical costs. And the burden on the families. Countless hours caring for them until they die of old age."

"And you believe this could happen?"

"Yes. I'm telling you an attack is coming."

The cellblock door opened, and Sarah heard a man speak to René. He nodded and turned back to her. "Your lawyer has just arrived. I'll get him."

René escorted an older, gray-haired gentleman to Sarah's cell. He wore a black suit and wire-rimmed glasses and was carrying a briefcase.

"Sarah, this is Monsieur Gérard Beauvais. He has been kind enough to come here tonight and represent you. Now, if you'll both excuse me," René said and walked away.

Sarah smiled at the stone-faced lawyer. "Thank you so much for coming. I really appreciate it."

"Yes, of course," he said curtly. "First of all, I charge 200 euros an hour for my services. Just so you know, I'm not volunteering my time."

"I understand. And money's no problem," she lied, knowing his legal fees would quickly drain all the cash in her backpack.

"Good. Now, the inspector told me you assaulted a police officer. Is that true?"

"Yes, but that's not why I hired you. I need you to stay here all night and make sure nothing happens to me."

His jaw dropped. "You're asking me to stay here *all night*?"

"That's correct. All night."

Sarah told her story, and Gérard listened intently. When she finished, he closed his eyes. "No, no, no. This is ridiculous," he said before opening them.

"First of all, you're in a police station. I can't think of a safer place. And second, I'm not a bodyguard. I've never even fired a gun. So, if someone really is determined to kill you and can get past all the policemen, what good will I be?"

"That's exactly why I hired you," Sarah replied. "To make sure no one gets past them. I need you to warn everyone here to be vigilant. And I need you to stay awake all night and make sure they don't lower their guard. Not for one second."

"I'm sorry, but I don't think—"

"*Please*. My life is in danger. You must help me."

Gérard stared at the floor.

"I've got no one else."

He mumbled a few words to himself and looked at her. "Okay."

She exhaled a sigh of relief. "Thank you. Tomorrow morning, after I talk to someone at the U.S. Embassy, I'll pay you, and you can leave. Okay?"

"Okay."

The lawyer reached into his briefcase and pulled out a clipboard that held a document. He filled in several blank spots and handed her the clipboard and pen.

"This is my contract. Again, it's 200 euros an hour for my services. I just need you to sign at the bottom."

"Sure," Sarah said and added her signature.

"Would you like me to speak to the officers now?"

"Yes. And after that, I need you to buy me a liter of water or juice and some energy bars."

"Okay."

She looked down at her splint. "And tell René I need my pain meds. They're in my backpack."

"Anything else?"

"No. But please hurry back."

———

Gérard returned carrying a shopping bag. "I explained your situation to the men on duty. They locked the front doors and will screen anyone wishing to gain entry."

"Oh, my god. Are you serious?"

"Yes."

Sarah broke a smile. "You have no idea how relieved I am to hear that."

"And I will stay awake all night and make sure they remain vigilant."

"Thank you so much. Please tell everyone how grateful I am."

"I will do so. And here are the items you requested." He handed her the shopping bag between the cell bars.

Sarah looked inside and saw four candy bars, her prescription pain pills, and a one-liter bottle containing an orange beverage. She removed the bottle and examined it. The words *Santé naturelle* were emblazoned on the label.

She looked at Gérard. "I'd like you to take a sip of this."

"Why?"

"To make sure it's okay."

He scoffed. "There's nothing wrong with our products. France is not some underdeveloped country."

"I realize that, but . . . I'm sorry, I don't know you. I only know there are some people outside this jail that want me dead. So please forgive me if I'm a bit paranoid."

"Now I understand. You're worried someone might have poisoned it."

"Yes."

"And you don't want to die."

"Correct."

"But it's okay if *I* die," Gérard said. "Of course. You're

from the United States, so you think your life is more valuable than mine."

"Spare me the Ugly American speech, okay? Again, I'm sorry. But if you just bought this bottle of 'happy water,' there should be nothing wrong with it."

"There *is* nothing wrong with it," he insisted. "For someone to inject a poison into that bottle, they would have to know you'd send me to a store. And they'd have to guess which store I'd choose. And then guess that I'd buy you a bottle of *Santé naturelle*. And even *which* bottle of *Santé naturelle* I'd buy. That would be impossible."

"I agree," Sarah said. "So, you should have no problem taking a drink. Unless you're working for them."

"I beg your pardon."

She extended the bottle toward him. "Just one sip."

Gérard glared at her. "No. You Americans come over here and throw dollars at our feet and expect us to dance. Well, I refuse to demean myself for your precious dollars. Goodbye."

The exasperated inspector reappeared at her cell. "I spent half an hour finding you a lawyer, and after just ten minutes with you, he quit."

"Where did you find him?"

"Online."

"I don't trust him."

"Of course not. You don't trust anyone."

"I need you to stay with me tonight."

René exhaled loudly. "No amount of money could entice me to do that. And I won't waste my time getting you another lawyer, either. I'm done." He turned and walked away.

"Wait," Sarah said. She held up the bottle of *Santé naturelle*. "Do you know what's in this?"

He stopped and looked back at her. "Yes. It's an energy drink. It has mineral water. Fruit juice. Vitamins. Antioxidants."

"You left out T-3."

"Excuse me?"

"Someone added T-3 to it. You drink this, and your brain will shut down."

René shook his head and offered a few choice words in French. "May I please see it?"

Sarah handed him the bottle through her jail cell door. He held it up and examined it under a fluorescent ceiling light. "It looks fine to me."

"Wow, your scientific police work is stunning."

He lowered the bottle and slowly rotated it. "The cap seal is not broken."

"That's because they injected T-3 into the bottle."

He turned it upside down and squeezed it with his hands. "As you can see, I'm applying a good amount of pressure. If someone punctured this bottle with a hypodermic needle, there should be a tiny hole somewhere. But I don't see any liquid escaping. Do you?"

From inside the facing cell, Lisette complained to René. He faced her, and they had a conversation.

"What's she saying?"

"She wants your *Santé naturelle*." He walked over to Lisette's cell and handed it to her.

"No!" Sarah said.

Lisette opened the bottle and took a sip.

"Don't drink that. *Lisette*, do not drink that!"

"I'm afraid she doesn't understand English," René said.

Lisette sat down on her bunk bed and drank from the bottle.

Sarah glared at René. "Do you have any idea what you just did? You're killing her!"

"Does she look like she's dying?"

"She has T-3 in her stomach. Its protective coating is breaking down as we speak. In a few minutes, the drug will enter her large intestine, get absorbed into the bloodstream, and make its way into her brain. Do you understand?"

René looked down and pulled a piece of lint from his slacks.

"If you want to save her life, you must induce vomiting."

He smirked.

"Goddammit, give her something to induce vomiting. Now!"

"No! I'm done taking orders from you," René responded with equal ferocity. "Your *Santé naturelle* is not poisoned. Lisette is not an assassin. Nor is your lawyer. People are not gathering outside to kill you. You're delusional. You don't need a lawyer; you need a psychiatrist." He walked away and slammed the cellblock door shut behind him.

Sarah let out a shriek and pounded the cell door. The sound echoed throughout the cellblock. She saw

Lisette sitting on the bunk bed, staring at her as she drank from the bottle of *Santé naturelle*.

"No," Sarah implored, shaking her head back and forth. "Don't drink that."

Lisette took a few more sips and screwed the cap on. She set the bottle on the floor and began fiddling with her hair. A minute later, she stretched her arms and lay down.

Sarah thought back on her arguments with the lawyer and René and wondered if the cumulative stress from this ordeal had caused her to overreact about the bottle of *Santé naturelle*.

Regardless, two things were certain: she'd lost her lawyer—the most important ally in her fight to survive the night—and Marcel and his flock of vultures were hovering outside. At this moment, alone and trapped in her eight-by-fourteen-foot cell, she felt more vulnerable than ever.

chapter twenty-one

———

Sarah heard the cellblock door open and watched a policeman carry a tray of food over to Lisette. She was asleep in the lower bunk bed. "Lisette. *Voici ton dîner*," he said.

She didn't respond, and Sarah's heart thumped.

"Lisette," the man said in a louder voice as he rattled her cell door. "*Voici ton dîner!*" Getting no reaction, he set the tray of food on the cement floor, slid it under the door to her cell, and went back upstairs.

"No, no. Please, no," Sarah whispered to herself. She remembered administering the PET scan to the mouse in Lab 131 and how the red, orange, and yellow images of its brain turned blue after she injected it with T-3.

"Lisette . . . Lisette!" She banged on her cell door, desperately trying to jar the woman awake.

"René, get down here! Hurry! Lisette's unconscious!"

The cellblock door crashed open, and René rushed

over to Lisette's cell and unlocked the door. He entered, kneeled beside her, and shook her ragdoll body.

"Lisette. *Réveille-toi . . . réveille-toi.*"

"What are you saying?"

"I'm trying to wake her up, but she's not responding."

Sarah squeezed a hunk of hair. "No! This can't be happening!" she cried out as tears welled in her eyes.

He got onto the mattress and began giving her chest compressions.

Unable to watch the macabre scene unfolding before her eyes, Sarah looked at the floor.

"Stop it, René. For god's sake, stop it! She doesn't need CPR. Her heart is beating."

He ignored her anguished words.

"René, *please*. It's too late. There's nothing you can do."

He snapped his head toward her. "And how do you know this?"

"Because I created the drug she ingested."

She heard footsteps in the stairwell and saw three police officers responding to the loud voices. René addressed them and pulled out his phone.

"Who are you calling?" Sarah demanded.

"Emergency services. She must get to a hospital."

"No . . . René, no! It doesn't matter if she gets to a hospital in ten minutes or ten hours. The damage is already done."

He glared at her. "If you don't mind, I'd like to hear that from a doctor."

"I *am* a doctor, goddammit! Would you *please* listen to me?"

René hesitated and then barked an order to the officers standing in the hallway. They disappeared up the stairs.

"Okay, I'm listening. You tell me what I should do."

"There's nothing you *can* do. It's too late."

"No, it's not too late," he insisted. "She's alive. I feel a pulse."

"Yes. She has a pulse. And she's breathing. But her brain is dead," Sarah said, choking up. "She's not coming back. She's gone."

Sarah buried her face in her hands and broke down. In between sobs and labored breaths, she whispered apologies to Lisette.

The shaken inspector watched Sarah cry and thought back to the moment she stormed into his life. She was desperate. Irrational. Crazy. And she wove the most incredible tale of intrigue. He turned back to Lisette, looked into her blank eyes, and was forced to concede that Sarah wasn't crazy after all.

He got to his feet, put his phone away, and walked over to her cell. Sarah continued her outpouring of grief for some time—until she was drained of emotion.

René reached a hand through the bars and gently squeezed her right shoulder. "I'm sorry," he said, "this is my fault."

She raised her head, sniffed, and wiped tears from her eyes. "It's not your fault. I created that drug."

"But if I'd listened to you, Lisette would be okay."

"It doesn't matter. What's important now is that you believe me. You saw what T-3 did to her."

"Yes."

"Now multiply that by a hundred. Or a thousand. Or ten thousand. You see what's coming."

"Yes. I'll call my supervisor right now and tell him what just happened."

"Whoever you call needs to pull together a meeting of your top people."

"I agree," René said. "Hopefully, he can arrange one tonight."

"Insist on it. We don't have much time. And send someone to Hôtel L'Impériale. The woman who's staying in Suite 404 is working for them."

"Okay. I'll send an undercover officer."

"Good," Sarah said. "And, by the way, I want to know where you got my lawyer."

He fidgeted. "Okay, I'll tell you the truth. I was trying to find you an English-speaking lawyer who would come here tonight. The first two I spoke with declined. Then a man called. He was looking for a woman named Sarah—an American who matches your description. I told him you'd been arrested for assaulting a police officer. He wasn't surprised. He said you have schizophrenia. When you stop taking your medications, you invent fantastic stories and think people are trying to kill you. You become violent."

"And you believed him?"

"Yes." René raised his hands as if surrendering. "I'm sorry, but he was describing you perfectly. And you did attack one of my officers, no?"

"Go on."

"Anyway, he said he couldn't bail you out because you believed he wanted to kill you. But he could send his lawyer. Hopefully, the lawyer would convince you to take your medications."

She bit her lip and stared at him with bloodshot eyes but said nothing.

"I'll be back," René said and walked away.

———

Sarah was pacing the floor when René returned and entered her cell. "I locked the front doors and put everyone on alert. I also talked to my supervisor. He was able to reach Gabriel Parmentier, the minister of the interior. Gabriel is organizing a meeting for tonight."

"Good," Sarah said. "And where will that meeting take place?"

"At his home in Domont, thirty kilometers north of here. Once everyone has gathered, I'll put you on speakerphone."

Sarah thought for a moment. "That won't be necessary."

"Why?"

"Because I'm going to the meeting."

René cocked his head.

"What number do you call for a medical emergency?"

"One-one-two."

"I need you to do it. When an ambulance shows up, Marcel and his guys will wonder what's going on."

"Who's Marcel?"

"He's in charge of their operation. Anyway, they'll see paramedics wheel me out of the station and know

I'm trying to escape. And what an ingenious plan, right? Everyone here thinks I'm crazy. But if I have an 'emergency,' an ambulance will rush me to a hospital. I'll be safe, and I can convince doctors I'm telling the truth."

René shook his head. "That's not a very good plan. If these people are as dangerous as you claim, they'll kill you before you reach the hospital."

"I know," Sarah said.

"Then I'm confused."

"The woman going to the hospital won't be me. It'll be Lisette."

He scoffed. "That's ridiculous. She doesn't look anything like you."

"Not right now, but she will. I'll cut off my braids and put them on her."

"You can't be serious."

"It's dark outside. They'll be watching from a distance, so they won't get a good look at her. If anything, they'll notice the braids. Meanwhile, I can walk out of here wearing a police uniform, get into a car, and drive away."

"You really think you can fool them?"

"I don't have to. I only need to distract them for a few seconds."

René looked over at Lisette and then turned back to Sarah. "You want to gamble with her life."

A tear rolled down her cheek. "Yes. I know that's terrible, but . . . she's not coming back. We can't help her. But she can help *me* get out of here."

"There's no reason for you to leave," René said.

"With all due respect, I don't feel safe. They'll figure out a way to get in here and kill me."

"Well, I'm confident we can protect you. But if you insist on leaving, allow me to suggest a better plan. I can get a commando squad here in fifteen minutes. They'll back up an armored vehicle to the front door, take you inside, and drive you to safety."

Sarah shook her head. "No. If Marcel sees the cavalry showing up, he'll know I have allies. They'd cover their tracks and go into hiding. We'd never catch them. And if Marcel isn't caught, I'll be looking over my shoulder for the rest of my life."

"I see your concern. So . . . let's go with your idea."

"Thanks. Can you get me a First Responder kit?"

"Yes."

"And I need a sharp pair of scissors." Sarah brought a hand up to her braid and stroked it.

René left and came back a minute later with a white case. He opened it for Sarah's inspection. It was filled with bandages, pads, alcohol wipes, latex gloves, and assorted paraphernalia. He took out a pair of scissors. "These are razor-sharp. They're for cutting off a person's clothing."

"Perfect," Sarah said and turned her back to him. "I need you to cut these off as close to my head as possible. Try to do a good job."

René gripped one of her braids, pulled it taut, and began snipping away. It put up resistance but was no match for the scissors.

"Okay, I cut off the first one," he said.

Sarah imagined her severed braid thrashing about in agony after losing its warm life support.

René held the remaining braid and cut through it in short order. "That's it. I'm done."

"Thank you," Sarah said and looked at Lisette. "I'm going to try very hard not to lose it."

"Lose what?" René asked.

"My composure."

They entered her cell, and Sarah sat on the lower bunk and cradled Lisette's head in her lap. She looked down at her face and burst into tears. "I am so sorry . . . I am so sorry," she said, caressing Lisette's forehead.

After some time, she looked at René and inhaled and exhaled a deep breath. "Okay, we have to do this."

She positioned the braids while René secured them to the back of Lisette's head with surgical tape. When he was finished, Sarah lowered Lisette's head down and eased away. She grabbed a few pads from the First Responder kit and placed them on Lisette's forehead. She then wrapped several layers of gauze around her head to hold the braids and the white pads in place. Finally, she secured the gauze with bandage clips.

Sarah turned to René. "Call for an ambulance. Tell them a prisoner fell and cracked her head open. And tell them she's lost a lot of blood."

———

Antoine Boucher, Collin Smith, and Gérard Beauvais huddled with Marcel under the jewelry store awning in Place Baudoyer. He waited for a church bell to stop ringing before addressing his men.

"Sarah is going to call the U.S. Embassy tomorrow morning. She could set forces into motion that will jeopardize this operation. And so, our task is clear. We must silence her before she can make that call." He looked at his watch. "We have thirteen hours."

Before he could continue, an emergency siren caught his attention. It grew louder. And louder. And then loud enough to drown out his voice. He looked in the direction of the noise and saw an ambulance. It drove into Place Baudoyer and backed up to the police station entrance. "Hôpital St. Vincent" was written on its side.

The driver turned off the siren and flashing lights, got out of the vehicle, and rushed through the front door. Two paramedics jumped out of the back of the ambulance, removed a gurney, and wheeled it inside the station.

"I believe Sarah is attempting an escape," Marcel said. "I'll go to St. Vincent Hospital and stake out a good position. Collin: I need you to put a tracker on the ambulance. You and Gérard follow it when it leaves. Antoine: You stay here and take pictures. I want everything that happens outside this station documented."

Sarah entered the women's restroom carrying a bulletproof vest and a uniform that René had given her. She avoided looking in the mirror, as she was not yet ready to see herself braid-less. She took off her street clothes and put on the Kevlar vest, a blue police uniform, a gun belt, a pair of shiny black shoes, and a cap. She left the bathroom, walked down the flight of stairs, and approached René. "How do I look?" she asked, tugging the cap snug over her forehead.

He gave her a once-over. "Taller."

"That's because I stuffed some paper towels into my shoes. I also tried to grow a beard, but . . ."

They both smiled, enjoying a moment of levity.

"My clothes are in the bathroom."

"That's fine."

"No, no. I need them. And my backpack."

"I'll make sure you get all of your belongings," René said. He turned and gave an order to one of his officers.

She saw three men putting on bulletproof vests similar to the one René had given her. "What's happening?"

"One of the paramedics has agreed to drive Lisette to the hospital. He'll be accompanied by two of my officers. They'll wear emergency services uniforms."

He pointed to a man struggling to pull a red *Service d'aide médicale urgente* shirt over his vest. "That muscular fellow is Benoit. He's skilled in martial arts and has combat experience in Mali. He'll ride in the back of the ambulance with Lisette."

"Good."

"In addition, I'll send two undercover men to St. Vincent Hospital. We'll be ready for an attack."

Sarah watched the paramedics lift Lisette off the bed and lower her onto a plastic backboard. "Wait a minute. Hold on," she said. "I need some blood."

The EMT who'd just loaned Benoit his uniform reached into a kit and removed a half-liter blood bag. Sarah took it from him, picked up a pair of scissors, and poked a hole near the top of the bag. She flipped the bag upside down and dangled it above Lisette's bandaged head. All eyes watched as blood trickled onto the gauze. She moved the bag in a circular motion, creating a large red stain on the white material. Satisfied with the result, Sarah turned the bag upright and handed it back to the EMT.

The paramedics secured Lisette to the backboard with straps and hoisted her off the ground.

René pulled Sarah aside. "Come with me." She followed him up the stairs and into his office. He walked over to his desk, unlocked a drawer, removed a pistol, and handed it to her.

Sarah examined the gun. "Is it loaded?"

"No."

"Are you kidding me?"

"Have you had firearms training?" René asked.

She shrugged. "Who cares?"

"I do. I won't put my men at risk."

"But it's okay to put *me* at risk?"

"You're wearing a bulletproof vest. And my officers will protect you."

"I understand that. But I still want to be able to defend myself."

"With a deadly weapon you've never even held before, much less been trained how to use?"

Sarah weighed his point. "You're right. I'm sorry."

"It's okay."

"Do you at least have some glasses I could borrow for a disguise?"

René reached inside a desk drawer and pulled out his reading glasses. "Make sure I get these back."

He got up, walked over to a supply closet, and took a blue jacket off its hanger. "See if this fits you."

She tried it on and gave him a thumbs-up.

They left his office, and he led her over to a young police officer. René spoke to the man before introducing her to him. "Sarah, this is Philippe. He'll drive you to the meeting."

"Great. What about my backpack and my clothes?"

"They're in a box in the trunk of his car."

René walked to a front window and parted the blinds. He saw a few onlookers standing near the ambulance and ordered two of his men to shoo them away. After they'd fulfilled their task, he turned around and surveyed the silent room: Lisette was lying on a gurney. Philippe, the paramedic, Sarah, and four police officers—two of them wearing EMT uniforms—were strategically positioned to shield her face.

René looked at Sarah. "Are you ready?"

She slid her hands into the jacket pockets and made sure her splinted finger was hidden. "Yes."

He opened the station doors and gave an "okay" sign. The paramedic wheeled Lisette outside while the others stayed in formation around the gurney. Sarah kept her head down to avoid making eye contact with Marcel or any members of his hit squad. René's glasses offered disguise but also skewed her vision and made it difficult to navigate the uneven pavement. She looked up and saw the paramedic push the gurney into the back of the ambulance.

"Let's go," Philippe said. They walked to a police car, and Sarah got in the passenger seat. To help conceal her face, she opened the glove compartment and pretended to search for something inside.

Philippe got behind the wheel, started the engine, and drove away from Place Baudoyer. Sarah closed the glove compartment and took off René's glasses and the police cap. She turned around and looked out the back window.

"Do you see anyone following us?"

"No."

"Get ready," Philippe said. He flipped on the siren and sped down a busy street. Sarah secured her seat belt and stared wide-eyed as he ran a red light. Then another. She stole a look at the speedometer. It read 87 kilometers per hour.

Philippe slammed the brakes to avoid T-boning a truck, and Sarah jerked forward. He swerved around the vehicle and stomped on the accelerator. Her back pressed against the seat as they zoomed forward.

Great. I escape from Marcel, only to be killed by my driver.

He slowed down, turned left, and made an immediate right onto a dark street. He shut off the siren, sped to the end of the block, did a U-turn, and pulled over to the curb.

"Get your head down," he said and switched off the headlamps and engine. She followed his order.

They sat still for two minutes. No cars drove by. No pedestrians appeared.

"I think we're okay," he said.

Sarah pushed herself up in her seat.

"So, is this your first visit to Paris?"

chapter twenty-two

———

Marcel parked his car, pulled an attaché case from the trunk, and walked toward St. Vincent Hospital. Nearing the emergency room entrance, he removed a pair of night-vision goggles from his suit jacket pocket, put them on, and looked for a good vantage point. An isolated position. Not too far away. Not too close.

After a quick search, he chose a hill approximately two hundred meters away—well beyond the row of businesses lining the opposite side of the street.

Marcel crossed Rue de Sèvres and jogged a sidewalk between two buildings to the back of the complex. He continued through a parking lot, stepped over a broken fence, and climbed the hill. After reaching the top, he looked around and found a prime spot behind a juniper tree. His phone rang.

"Hello?"

"You were right," Antoine said. "Sarah is trying to escape. They just put her in the ambulance."

"I'll be ready when she arrives," Marcel said.

He set his attaché case on the ground and opened it. While assembling the rifle, he remembered training as a young man under the tutelage of Arkady Volkov. The storied marksman had taught him how to calculate the trajectory of a fired bullet based on many factors—the type of rifle and ammunition used, distance and elevation from the target, and weather conditions. After much practice, he'd conquered the science and, as a professional assassin, prided himself on hitting his victim in the heart. It always guaranteed a quick kill and—more often than not—surprisingly little blood loss.

In contrast, shooting someone in the head or elsewhere in the upper torso was messy and could be excruciatingly painful for the recipient. He respected his targets and didn't want to torture or humiliate them. And he respected the medical personnel who would arrive at the scene. Why make their job more unpleasant? His goal was always an immediate kill and a minimum amount of gore.

A siren interrupted his thoughts and forced him to focus on the task at hand. He finished assembling his M4 carbine assault rifle and made sure it was ready for use. The siren grew louder and then went silent as the ambulance came into view and pulled up in front of the emergency room entrance.

Marcel raised his rifle, peered through its scope, and

watched the EMTs open the back doors of the vehicle and remove the gurney. Their patient had a bandaged forehead. And braids.

He held his breath, took aim, and squeezed the trigger. He heard the shot and felt a kick to his right shoulder. Through the riflescope, he saw her body jerk as a 5.56 mm bullet ripped through her heart.

———

Philippe and Sarah left behind the bright lights of Paris and headed north. In thirty minutes, they reached Domont. Philippe turned off Rue de la République and onto a dark, two-lane road. He rounded a curve and pulled into a driveway alongside three other cars in front of a two-story house.

"We're here," Philippe said. He shut off the engine, popped the trunk latch, and got out of the car. Sarah retrieved her backpack from the trunk and saw a bald man wearing blue jeans and an untucked white dress shirt approach Philippe and engage him in conversation. She walked over to them, and the man looked at her and extended his hand.

"Hi, Sarah. Welcome to Domont. I'm Interior Minister Gabriel Parmentier."

They exchanged a firm handshake. "It's nice to meet you," she said. "Thank you for arranging this meeting on such short notice."

Gabriel led his guests through the front door of his home. Sarah entered the living room and was struck by the combination of new and old. A flat-screen television sat on a nineteenth-century table. Track lighting illuminated paintings by French masters. Wireless speakers played Mozart's *Eine Kleine Nachtmusik*.

"I'd like you to meet my wife, Anne-Marie," Gabriel said. Sarah turned to a tall, thin woman. She was dressed in black suede pants and an azure top that complemented her silver hair.

Anne-Marie smiled and shook Sarah's hand. "*Enchantée*. I understand you've had quite an adventure."

Sarah nodded her head slowly. "I guess that's one way to put it."

"We're just waiting for a representative from your embassy," Gabriel noted. "He should be here soon. In the meantime, Anne-Marie will show you to your accommodation."

"I'm staying here tonight?" Sarah asked.

"Yes."

"Please come with me," Anne-Marie said and escorted Sarah up a flight of stairs and into a second-floor bedroom. "I hope this is okay."

Sarah looked up at the timbered ceiling and then lowered her gaze to admire the stone fireplace, abstract art paintings, Persian rugs, and, last but not least, the king-size bed.

"It's perfect."

"And you have your own bathroom," Anne-Marie said, pointing to a door with a little WC sign hanging on it. "Is there anything I can get you?"

Sarah considered her offer. "Well, now that you ask, I haven't eaten since lunch. So, if I could just grab a little—"

"Yes, of course. Do you eat beef?"

"I eat everything."

"Good. I'll prepare you some dinner."

"Please, don't go out of your way."

"I'm not," Anne-Marie said and left the room.

Sarah walked into the bathroom feeling a mixture of curiosity and apprehension and looked in the mirror. Her heart sank. She had almost no hair. And a tiny head. And her face was shockingly pallid. Could it be that her braids—or the long, curly locks she wore when her hair was unbraided—made her look more attractive than she really was? Assuming she could patch things up with Rogelio, what would he think? Would she still bring an amorous smile to his face?

She laid her backpack on the vanity, opened its main compartment, and was happy to see her running shoes and the cargo pants and top she'd worn at the police station. She felt the side pocket of the pants to make sure the syringe of Entoryl-XT was still there.

Sarah changed into her own clothes, swallowed two pain pills with a glass of water, and examined herself in the mirror again. She left the bedroom and went downstairs. Anne-Marie was waiting for her.

"Your dinner is ready," she said and led Sarah into the kitchen. "Please sit down."

She took a seat at a table with a formal place setting and watched Anne-Marie press buttons on a microwave oven. A minute later, she removed a plate of food and brought it over. It contained a sizzling steak, scalloped potatoes, and green beans.

"That looks wonderful," Sarah said and bent over to

savor the aroma. Anne-Marie poured her a glass of red wine and pulled a bottle of Perrier from the refrigerator.

"Thank you so much. I apologize for the imposition."

Anne-Marie shrugged. "It's not an imposition at all. We rarely have guests, so it's my pleasure." She gestured at the plate of food. *"Bon appétit."*

Sarah began scarfing down her dinner while Anne-Marie puttered about the kitchen. Neither spoke until Sarah sat back in her chair and looked at the empty plate.

"Wow. That was delicious," she said.

"Would you care for some more?"

"Not right now."

"Okay. There's plenty in the refrigerator should you get hungry."

"Thanks. I really appreciate it," Sarah said and finished off her glass of wine. "So, did Gabriel tell you why we're meeting here tonight?"

"No, but it must be important. He never schedules meetings for Sunday night."

"You're right; it is important. It's all because of me."

"Congratulations."

Sarah shook her head. "No. I did something dangerous. Something I shouldn't have done. Now I need his help."

Anne-Marie smiled. "Well, I'm sure everything will be okay."

"I guess we'll find out," Sarah said. She examined the splint, squeezed it, and winced.

"What happened to your hand?" Anne-Marie asked.

"Some guy broke my finger."

"Oh, no."

"It's okay. Have you heard the expression, 'you reap what you sow'?"

"Yes. It's from the Bible."

Sarah furrowed her eyebrows. "I didn't know that. When I was a little girl, I thought it had something to do with farming. Then my dad told me it means 'payback's a bitch.' You ever heard that one?"

Anne-Marie laughed. "No, I cannot say that I have." Her smile faded, and she assumed a curious expression. "And, if I may ask, what happened to your hair?"

"I told the inspector to cut off my braids. How does it look?"

"Mmm, not so good."

"Oh, well. That's the least of my worries."

Gabriel came into the kitchen and approached his wife. "*Ma chérie*. I'm sorry, but I must speak with Sarah in private."

"Of course," Anne-Marie said. She picked up a glass of wine and walked away.

He came over to the table and looked into her eyes. "Lisette was murdered."

Sarah gasped.

"She was shot by a sniper outside of St. Vincent Hospital."

"Did they catch the killer?"

"No. Unfortunately, René's undercover officers were stationed near the entrance. The sniper was a long distance away."

"Shit."

"Anyway, Dan has arrived. We should go ahead and start the meeting."

Sarah accompanied Gabriel into the dining room, where three men were seated around a large table. He introduced her to Dan Spishock, head of security at the U.S. Embassy, and to Jacque Lefèvre and André Brun, French intelligence agents. Following a round of pleasantries, Sarah and Gabriel sat down.

"If there's no objection, I'll turn it over to Sarah," he said. "She can explain why we're gathered here tonight."

With all eyes focused on her, she described the fateful experiment and the stunning chain of events that followed—culminating with the tragedy of Lisette. She finished on an ominous note: "They know how to produce an ingestible T-3. I believe their plan was to test it on Paul and me first. To make sure it works and to silence us. Then they'd carry out their real attack. When, where, and against whom? I don't know. But an attack is coming."

After fielding some questions, André slid his laptop over to her. "I just accessed our criminal database and did a search using three criteria: male, over the age of fifty, and currently unincarcerated. Perhaps you could look through these photos? You might recognize this 'Marcel' fellow."

"Sure." Sarah said. She began scrolling through the mug shots one by one, keeping in mind that he might have changed his appearance. She flipped through fat faces. Thin faces. Handsome faces. Cringe-worthy faces.

Seven minutes and 341 mug shots later, she leaned

back in her chair and sighed. "No luck. I didn't see him."

"So, we still don't know who Marcel is," Gabriel said.

"No. But he's in Paris."

"How do you know?"

She remembered his chilling words before she collapsed to the sidewalk in Redwood City: "At this very moment, I have the crosshairs of my riflescope fixed on you."

"Because he shot Lisette. You have to catch him before he disappears. And we have to find Paul because they're going to kill him next."

"I agree," Gabriel said.

"I'm also worried about my boyfriend. Marcel might target him too."

"Sarah," Dan said, "give me his information, and I'll contact the FBI. They'll put him in protective custody."

"They can do that?" she asked.

"Yes. Now, as for Paul," Dan continued, "I think we should call him."

"No," Gabriel said. "We could put his life in danger."

"I realize that. But what's our alternative?"

"I'll submit a request to ping his phone. We'll learn his exact location."

"*If* Paul has his locate feature turned on. And we'll have to wait for court approval. He could be dead by then. We need to call him *now*. At least he'll have a fighting chance to survive."

The room was quiet as everyone considered Dan's bold proposal.

Sarah shot both hands up. "I just thought of something." Using André's laptop, she Googled NYU School of Medicine and brought up Paul Johansen's homepage. She read a paragraph in his biography that noted he'd won a national science prize while attending high school in Ardmore, Pennsylvania.

She did a search for everyone in the Ardmore area with the last name of Johansen. There were five listings, including a Clare Johansen, aged sixty-seven. She pulled out her phone, entered 0-0-1, the Ardmore area code, and the phone number. After hearing a ring, she pressed the speaker button and set her phone on the table. A woman answered.

"Hi. Is this Clare Johansen?"

"Yes."

"Are you related to Paul?"

"May I ask who's calling?"

"I'm sorry. My name is Dr. Sarah Brenalen. I worked with him at MEREIN in California."

"I see. Yes, I'm his mother."

"Great. I'm so glad we connected. And let me just say that Paul is one of my heroes."

"Well, thank you. That's very kind," Clare said.

"I'm wondering if you've been in contact with him recently."

"Yes. We talked this morning."

"Oh, okay. I was told he's vacationing somewhere in the Caribbean."

"He's in Barbados."

"Awesome. And do you know where he's staying?"

Sarah heard nothing from the other end.

"I need to get in touch with him. It's very important."

"Then why don't you give me your contact information. I'll let him know you called."

"Can you just tell me where he's staying?"

"I'm sorry, I'd rather not," Clare replied. "But I'd be happy to pass along a message."

Sarah gave Dan a "you take over" stare, and he nodded.

"Excuse me, ma'am. My name is Dan Spishock, and I'm with the United States Embassy in France. We're calling you from Paris. Please don't hang up. We need your help."

chapter twenty-three

Rogelio left Total Health & Fitness after his Sunday afternoon workout and was unlocking the door to his truck when he heard someone call his name. He turned and saw a young man wearing jeans and a San Francisco Giants jersey walking toward him.

"Yeah?"

The man pulled a wallet from a back pocket, flipped it open, and displayed a gold badge. "Matt Jamison, FBI Undercover. I'd like to talk to you."

Rogelio grew queasy. "Is this about Sarah?"

"Yes."

"Is she okay?"

"She's in custody."

"In custody?"

"Apparently, she got herself into some trouble."

"What kind of trouble?"

"I don't know."

"Fuck!" Rogelio blurted out and pounded the driver's side door with his fist. He paced back and forth a couple of times and then stopped and looked at Matt.

"Where is she?"

"I couldn't tell you."

"You don't know, or you're not telling me?"

"I honestly don't know her location."

"But she's in trouble?"

"That's my understanding."

Rogelio rubbed his forehead. "I need to sit down."

He opened the driver's side door to his pickup, sat down, and stared at the pavement.

"Are you okay?" Matt asked.

"No. I'm *not* okay," Rogelio shot back. "I'm trying to wrap my brain around this."

"Gotcha."

He shook his head and exhaled loudly. "This is un-believable. I mean, five days ago everything was fine. Or so I thought. And then, she took off. I thought she was depressed. I never would have guessed she did anything illegal. Never. Not Sarah."

He looked up at the agent. "Can I talk to her?"

"Not yet. I'm sorry, but this is still an active investigation."

"That's okay. I understand. I appreciate you coming over here to tell me."

"Actually, I didn't come here just to tell you about Sarah. We're worried someone might try to kill you."

Rogelio scrunched his eyebrows. "*What?* I didn't do anything."

"It doesn't matter. Sometimes innocent people get caught up in these things and—"

"What are you saying? She dragged me into her mess?"

"What I'm saying is . . . I want you to come with me."

———

Paul Johansen was enjoying a prime rib dinner and a glass of red wine at Las Palmas. He glanced up at the man and woman holding hands at a nearby table and wished he'd invited Erika to dinner when they crossed paths at the beach. This intimate cafe overlooking the Caribbean, with its candlelit tables and soft background music, would have been a perfect place to bring her. He decided not to dwell on it. After all, she'd soon be sharing his couch.

After eating dinner, he walked a quarter mile back to Paradise Cove Resort and entered his suite. He went into the bathroom, flipped the light switch, and gasped. A maid stood next to the shower; her right index finger pressed against her lips. She wore a beige uniform and held a sign that read, "My name is Marifer. I'm a police officer. Don't say a word. Your life is in danger."

———

Erika DuBois entered Paul's suite carrying a shopping bag and looked around. "Nice place."

"It's a bit pricy, but I like it."

"I brought Manhattan ingredients and some popcorn. I hope you have a microwave."

"I do."

She frowned. "What's that music?"

"Mahler's *Fourth Symphony*. If you'd prefer something else, just let me know."

"It's okay for now. Are you ready for a Manhattan?"

"Oh, yes."

Erika walked into the kitchen, set her shopping bag on the counter, and removed two bottles of liquor and a jar of cherries. "I need a couple of glasses and some ice."

"Coming right up," Paul said. He pulled an ice cube tray from the freezer and found two cocktail glasses in the cupboard.

Erika opened the bottle of rye and looked at him. "I'm sorry. I don't mean to be rude, but my parents played that music when I was a little girl. It brings back unpleasant memories. Could you put on something different?"

"Sure," he replied and left the kitchen. Erika pulled a vial from her purse and emptied its contents into Paul's glass. The classical music stopped and was replaced by smooth jazz. She returned the vial to her purse, poured a good amount of rye into both glasses, and added vermouth, ice, and a cherry. She carried the drinks into the living room and saw Paul sitting on the couch.

"Is this music a little better?"

"Yes, it's very nice. Thank you." She sat down next to Paul and handed him his Manhattan.

"So, where are you from?" he asked.

"Paris."

"Paris. The most beautiful city in the world."

Erika twitched her lips. "Well, I would say it used to be. But not anymore."

"No?"

"No. It's becoming a Third World city."

"In what sense?"

"I'd rather not talk about it. I just want to enjoy the evening."

"Okay," Paul said.

"And what about you?" she asked.

"I live in New York. Manhattan."

"Perfect. The same name as your drink. I hope you like it."

"I'm sure I will."

"Wait," Erika said. She set her drink down on the coffee table and pulled out her phone. "I want to take a photo of you."

"No," Paul protested. "I really hate getting my picture taken."

"It's just a holiday memory. Please?"

He reluctantly held up his Manhattan, and she took a photograph.

"Beautiful. And let me get one of you sipping it."

"Hold on. We have to do a toast."

Erika hesitated. "Okay." She put her phone down, and they each raised their drink.

"To new friends and adventures," Paul declared.

"*Pour ta santé*," Erika said as they clinked glasses. "It means 'to your health.' Now, a photo of you tasting your Manhattan."

"Okay. But first, I have a confession to make."

"A confession?"

"Yes. I told you I was staying here by myself. That's not true."

Erika offered a confused smile. "What?"

"Marifer. Would you like to come in and say hello?"

She stepped into the room, and Erika's smile disappeared when she noticed that the policewoman was pointing a gun at her face.

———

Marcel entered his room at the Mandarin Palace Hotel, walked over to the fully stocked bar, and poured himself a shot of Glenlivet. He'd just killed Sarah, so a celebratory drink was in order. He raised his crystal glass. "To my worthy opponent," he said and downed the single malt Scotch.

She was dead. And Paul? Marcel looked at his watch. It was 1:28 a.m.—7:28 p.m. in Barbados. He wondered if Erika had completed her mission.

Thirty kilometers to the north, in the sleeping town of Domont, Gabriel Parmentier received a call from Jorell Gonsalves, a police captain from Bridgetown, Barbados. Gabriel set his phone down on the mahogany table.

"Go ahead, Jorell. You're on speakerphone. What can you tell us?"

"First of all, I'm happy to report that Paul is okay. And we have in custody a thirty-year-old woman who offered him a suspicious cocktail. Her name is Erika Du-Bois. She's a French national and resides in Paris. Would you like to speak to her?"

"Yes. Give us a minute," Gabriel said as he, Jacque, and André simultaneously conducted searches on their laptops for any criminal records for a thirty-year-old Parisian named Erika DuBois. Gabriel pulled up her seven-page dossier and skimmed through it, occasionally scribbling notes on a piece of paper.

"We can all hear you," Jorell said, breaking what was perhaps a one-minute lull in the conversation. "Go ahead when you're ready."

"Okay, I think we should proceed," Gabriel said. He looked at his colleagues, as if waiting for permission to begin the questioning.

"Hello, Erika. My name is Gabriel Parmentier. I'm the interior minister of France. With me are security agents Jacque Lefèvre and André Brun, Dr. Sarah Brenalen, and a Mr. Spishock from the U.S. Embassy in Paris. I'd like to ask you a few questions. First, have you heard of the drug T-3?"

Erika didn't respond.

"Okay, next question. Who is Marcel?"

Silence.

"Dr. Brenalen said he forced her to give him a T-3 sample. Do you know why?"

Silence.

"I just read your police file. It says you're a member of *Patrie et Liberté*. Were you planning to reproduce the drug and attack immigrants?"

Again, no reply.

"You should know that two of your cohorts are co-operating with us in exchange for lesser charges."

Sarah shot Gabriel a quizzical look, and he shook his head.

Eight thousand kilometers to the west, on the other end of the phone call, Erika sat on a couch in Paul's vacation suite with her wrists handcuffed behind her back. Jorell's phone lay in front of her on the glass tabletop. Marifer, Jorell, and two other police officers stood guard while Paul paced the floor.

"Regarding your file," Gabriel continued, "it also notes you're a single mother raising a four-year-old daughter. Is that true?"

Silence.

"Four. What a wonderful age. I bet you love to hold her. Play games with her. Teach her things. It would be devastating if you could no longer do that. Imagine your beautiful little girl being ripped away from your arms. She'd be hysterical, not knowing why. And she'd be told you didn't love her anymore. And that—because you did terrible things—you'd be going to prison for many years, and she'd have to live in an orphanage."

Erika rocked slightly and stared ahead.

"It's getting late here in France, and I'm tired. So, if you're not going to answer any of my questions, let's just end this one-way conversation."

Silence.

"Before I hang up, is there anything you'd like to tell me? Anything at all?"

At that moment, a musical jingle rang out. All eyes in Paul's suite homed in on Erika's phone, which also lay on the glass table.

"She's receiving a call," Jorell said.

"Can you see the number?"

He crouched down to get a closer view. "It's an international call." He read aloud all thirteen digits.

"Interesting," Gabriel said. "Someone is calling her from Paris."

———

Marcel received a text message with one word: "Done." Attached were three photographs. The first showed Paul sitting on a couch and holding a drink. In the second photo, he was taking a sip. The third showed him sprawled on the couch, his eyes closed.

Marcel poured a second shot of Glenlivet and called George, the man in charge of the operation.

"We're done," he announced triumphantly.

"You got both of them?" George asked.

"Yes. In fact, Paul just received a dose of T-3."

"Where is he?"

"In a hotel room in Bridgetown."

"Good," George said. "After he's taken to a hospital, have one of your people claim to be a close friend, and request medical updates."

"Hospitals only divulge that information to family members," Marcel noted.

"Then he should strike up a relationship with one of Paul's relatives. Or plant a listening device in his hospital room. Either way, we must confirm there's no recovery from T-3—even with the best medical intervention."

"I agree."

"And what about Sarah?"

"She's dead. I shot her." Marcel replied.

"*What?* You told me Gérard was going to give her a tainted bottle of water."

"He did, but she wouldn't drink it."

"So . . . you *shot* her?"

"I had no choice. After Gérard left the jail, she suffered a head wound—self-inflicted, I believe—and was rushed to a hospital. I killed her as she was being wheeled inside."

"Wait a minute. You think she injured herself so that she'd be taken to a hospital?"

"Yes."

"That doesn't make sense," George said. "Why would she do such a thing?"

"She felt unsafe in her cell."

"So, in other words, she was saying, 'Hey Marcel, I know you're trying to kill me. But don't worry about getting inside this jail. I'll do you a favor and injure myself. An ambulance will come, and paramedics will take me outside. I'll be an easy target.'"

"Again, her plan was—"

"Until now, Sarah's been meticulous. I cannot believe she'd voluntarily put herself in such a vulnerable position."

"I'm telling you she was desperate to leave that jail."

"And you're sure it was Sarah you killed?"

"I'm sure of it. Why?"

"Because she's outwitted us before."

"Not this time," Marcel assured his boss.

"Okay, I believe you. Anyway, we have a lot to discuss, but it's getting late and I'd like to get some sleep."

"Yes, of course. I won't take any more of your time. Let's talk in the morning."

Marcel ended the call, downed his second shot of

Scotch, and sat on the edge of the bed. He bent over to untie his shoes but paused before his fingers reached the laces. Self-doubt was beginning to gnaw at him as he replayed his discussion with George.

While confident he'd disposed of Sarah, he none-theless walked over to the dresser and powered up his iPad Pro. He opened his email, flipped through An-toine's photos from Place Baudoyer, and stopped at one showing Sarah lying on a gurney just outside the police station. She was covered chest down with a white sheet, her upper body inclined, her head resting on a pillow. Bloody bandages covered her forehead, and her eyes were closed. An EMT blocked part of her face, but he saw the braids—the unmistakable braids he'd admired during their meeting at San Gregorio Beach—and knew it was Sarah.

But then, just before he turned off the tablet, some-thing about the photo caught his attention. Something he hadn't noticed before. He stroked his chin and stud-ied the image.

It came to him like a blow to the stomach.

Marcel opened his web browser and typed, "What is the length of an ambulance gurney." The answer: 213 centimeters.

He did a search for "Ambulances." The website for a company that produces them was one of the options that appeared on his screen. He clicked on it, scrolled down to the technical data of their newest emergency vehicle, and read that its gurney measured 65 by 215 centimeters.

Marcel now had two different answers for a gurney's

length. He split the difference and decided that Sarah's gurney was 214 centimeters long.

He opened his mathematical functions application, selected the square grid pattern, and superimposed it onto the photo. He dragged the pattern to the left until one of the vertical lines intersected the top of Sarah's head. He then counted the number of squares to the tips of her toes, which protruded up from beneath the white sheet. A tad over fourteen squares.

Marcel moved the grid pattern to the left until a vertical line intersected the top of the gurney. He counted the number of squares to its other end. It measured nineteen squares.

He brought up his calculator and did the math.

$14.1 \div 19 \times 214 = 158.8$

Hoping he'd somehow entered the wrong numbers, he redid his math but got the same answer. He grimaced and stared at the screen in disbelief.

The woman lying on the gurney was rather short—approximately 159 centimeters. Sarah, on the other hand, was *not* short. Based on their interactions, he knew she was almost his height—178 centimeters.

A wave of incredulity washed over him as he conceded that the woman in the photograph—this woman he'd shot outside of St. Vincent Hospital—was not Sarah.

He reviewed the photos that Antoine had sent him and counted eight people—the woman on the stretcher, three paramedics, and four police officers. One of the paramedics had dark skin and a beard. Even Hollywood couldn't transform Sarah in that brief amount of time. The second paramedic was tall. The third was short and stocky. He ruled them out.

Of the four cops, two went back inside the station. The other two got into a police car and drove away. In one of Antoine's photographs, they could be seen walking toward the car, their backs to the camera. He looked at the photo and noticed an interesting detail. The two officers wore matching uniforms and were the same height. Yet there was a subtle difference between them. The one on the left had a man's butt. The officer to his right had a pear-shaped, or—as he preferred to call it—upside-down heart-shaped *derrière* of a woman.

He flipped to the next photo. In it, the female officer was looking at her partner. He enlarged the image and could see that she wore glasses and had short hair.

Marcel then noticed the back of the woman's head, and his jaw dropped. He enlarged the image further and zoomed in on her botched haircut.

"Sarah," he whispered to himself.

He looked away from the tablet and remembered his prophetic warning to Collin: "Underestimate her at your peril."

Starting to panic, he debated whether to call George. He decided to wait until morning to deliver the grim news. In the meantime, he'd try to come up with a plan to salvage their mission.

As he struggled for ideas, he remembered that Collin had placed transmitters on three vehicles in Place Baudoyer—an ambulance and two police cars. He opened his GPS application and saw two flashing white dots on the Paris map. One was near St. Vincent Hospital. The second was in Place Baudoyer.

He expanded the Paris map and exhaled a sigh of relief. He even smiled.

There it was. The third flashing dot. Just outside of Paris in the town of Domont.

chapter twenty-four

———

Sarah took a shower and put on the silk robe Anne-Marie had provided her. She was preparing for bed when she heard a knock at the door. "Sarah, it's me. I have good news."

She recognized Gabriel's voice and opened the door. "You got Marcel?"

"No, but we've tracked him through his phone to a hotel room in Paris. A commando unit is being mobilized as we speak."

Despite her fatigue, she managed to smile. "Oh, my god. That's wonderful news."

"And I wanted you to know that the FBI contacted your friend Rogelio. They'll make sure nothing happens to him."

"Great." Her exuberant expression quickly morphed into one of concern. "What did they tell him?"

"Nothing."

"Can I talk to him?"

Gabriel shook his head. "Wait until we have Marcel in custody."

That was not the answer she was hoping to hear, but she decided not to press the issue.

"Oh, and Philippe will be on guard all night outside your bedroom."

Sarah poked her head into the hallway and saw him sitting in a chair and reading something on his phone.

"Any questions before I retire for the evening?"

"No," she replied. "Just . . . thank you for everything you've done."

He smiled. *"Dors bien, et rêve de belles choses."*

"You, too. Whatever that means."

He walked down the hall, entered a room, and closed the door.

Philippe got up from his chair and came over to her. "Can I see your phone? I want you to have my number."

"Sure," Sarah said and handed it to him.

He entered his information and gave it back to her. "I'm now in your contacts. Philippe Montserrat. Call me if you need anything."

"Thanks, I will."

He pulled out a pack of Gauloises cigarettes. "I'm going outside for a break. Would you care to join me?"

Sarah's eyes lit up. Smoking a cigarette would soothe her nerves and provide an excuse to celebrate Marcel's imminent capture. Just one cigarette. Then she thought about her happy lungs and forced herself to decline his offer.

"No thanks. I don't smoke."

"That's good," Philippe said. He held up the pack of Gauloises. "These things will kill you."

———

At 2:37 a.m., the four commandos of the elite *Brigade de recherche et d'intervention*, each armed and wearing body armor, stood in the lighted hallway outside Room 916 of the Mandarin Palace Hotel.

Commando Two prepared his one-million-lumen floodlight for use. Bowing to objections from the night manager, this weapon was chosen over a standard flash grenade, which would send shock waves throughout the hotel. *BriteyWhitey*, on the other hand, would momentarily blind anyone in the room without startling any of the other 561 well-heeled guests.

The "light man" looked at his comrades-in-arms and indicated that he was ready. The four secured protective goggles over their eyes and gave each other a thumbs-up. So began "Operation Do Not Disturb."

Commando One slid a card into the room's key slot and heard a beep. He swung the door open, dove inside, and pulled his Glock 19 handgun.

Commando Two followed him in and engulfed the premises in white light.

Commandos Three and Four came in standing and scoured the bedroom through the scope of their respective assault rifles.

The room was a no-show, its unmade bed the only indication that someone had been staying there. They conducted a thorough search of all the rooms and closets before regrouping and acknowledging that they were too late. Marcel had disappeared.

———

Antoine Boucher parked on the shoulder of the two-lane road, got out of his car, and walked fifty feet to the darkened house. He saw two vehicles in the driveway. One of them had "POLICE" written in blue letters on its passenger-side door. He pulled out his phone and texted Marcel.

As instructed, he crept around the side of the house to the backyard and saw a tiny, white light pulsating in the blackness. He squeezed between a fence and a row of shrubs, tiptoed toward the light source, and soon recognized his partner. Marcel was kneeling on the ground and holding a flashlight. Antoine walked over to him and squatted down.

"She's here," he said, just loud enough to be heard over the din of crickets. "A policeman drove her from Paris. He's guarding her right now."

Antoine stood and looked over the top of the neatly trimmed hedge that provided cover. He surveyed the house, a mere stone's throw away, and crouched down again. "Do you know who lives there?"

"No."

"So, what's the plan?"

"The *policier* comes outside every half hour or so to smoke a cigarette. When he's done, he enters a code on a keypad. That probably disables the security alarm and unlocks the door. Then he goes back inside.

"On his next break, after he disables the alarm and

opens the door, I'll shoot him. Then I'll grab hold of the door before it closes and enter the house."

Antoine considered Marcel's plan. "That's a big house. How do you expect to find her?"

"There's a room on the second floor with the lights on. I believe she's staying there."

"How do you know?"

"I saw a silhouette in the curtains. I'm quite sure it was her."

"Okay. And what do you want me to do?"

"After I enter the house, keep an eye on the *policier* and make sure he doesn't get up. And if by chance Sarah eludes me and runs out the back door, I want you to kill her."

———

Sarah kept falling asleep, only to wake up with a jolt. Serenaded by crickets and cooled by a breeze that delivered fresh air through the partially open window, she inhaled and exhaled a deep breath and turned onto her side.

As she began to fall back to sleep, an unexpected noise shattered the tranquility. The noise was followed by a grunt. She snapped to attention and heard more sounds that seemed out of place at this hour. Her heart raced.

Sarah leapt out of bed and called Philippe. His phone rang. Then a second time. And a third time.

"Answer your fucking phone," she implored and began pacing the darkened room. After the fourth ring, she heard Philippe's voicemail greeting.

She wanted to shout out to him—and to Gabriel and Anne-Marie—but knew that doing so would announce her location to a potential killer. Then she remembered the phone number for emergency services and called it. A female voice answered and said words Sarah didn't understand.

"Do you speak English?" she asked in a hushed voice.

"Yes. What's your emergency?"

"Some people are breaking into the house. They're going to kill me. I don't know the address, but I'm staying in Gabriel Parmentier's home. He's your interior minister."

"Give me one moment," the operator said and put her on hold.

Sarah ran into the bathroom, threw on her clothes, and crept to the bedroom door to make sure that it was locked. She heard footsteps coming from the hallway and saw the doorknob twist back and forth.

"Okay, ma'am," came from her phone. "Officers have been dispatched. I'll stay on the line . . ."

Sarah muted the phone and held her breath. Three muffled pops broke the silence, and she shrieked. The bedroom door now had a jagged hole near the doorknob, projecting a beam of light from the hallway. A gloved hand came through the opening and reached for the lock.

She ran to the fireplace, grabbed an iron poker, and headed for the bathroom.

———

Marcel slid a hand through the hole in the door, felt for the locking mechanism, and turned it. He eased open the door and stepped inside the bedroom. Holding a semi-automatic handgun in his right hand, he pulled a flashlight from a jacket pocket with his left hand and shined it around the room.

"Philippe! Gabriel! Anne-Marie! Someone's in the house!" he heard Sarah scream. He trained his gun and flashlight on a door with a WC sign and riddled it with bullets. He walked over to the door and, after unsuccessfully trying to turn the handle, stepped back and gave it a swift kick. A piece of moulding broke free and fell to the floor. He kicked the door again, and it flung open. With his gun extended, he aimed the flashlight into the bathroom. He saw no one but heard a female voice: "Ma'am, can you talk? Hello?"

Marcel pointed his gun at a closet door and fired several rounds into it. He took three steps into the bathroom, opened the closet, and saw shelves with neatly folded towels and sheets. A cell phone, its screen lit, lay on one of the stacks of towels. "Please, ma'am, I need to know if you're okay," came from the phone.

Before he could curse her and spin around, a powerful blow struck the side of his head and sent him crumpling to the floor.

Sarah dropped the fireplace poker, reached down, and grabbed one of Marcel's legs. She jabbed the syringe filled with Entoryl-XT into his quad muscle and pushed the plunger.

Marcel raised his pounding head off the floor and wiped blood from his left eye. He aimed his gun at her and shot twice. She flew backward and hit the ground with a thud. He savored victory for two seconds before his eyes closed and he lost consciousness.

———

Anne-Marie was jarred awake by a frantic plea for help. She shook her husband. "Gabriel. Wake up. I think Sarah's in danger."

Gabriel opened his eyes as loud, disturbing noises came from the adjacent room. He flung off bed covers, opened a nightstand drawer, and pulled out a gun. "Get in the closet," he whispered to Anne-Marie.

———

Sarah heard the singsong wail of a French emergency vehicle. It grew louder, hit a crescendo, and then went silent. The pain in the left side of her chest intensified as she got to her feet and ran out of the bedroom. She made it down the stairs, opened the front door, and saw four police officers.

"Sarah, are you okay?" came a voice from behind.

She spun around and saw Gabriel in his pajamas, holding a gun.

"I don't know."

"Where's Philippe?" he asked.

"The last time I saw him, he was going outside to smoke a cigarette."

Gabriel ran into the kitchen and switched on the lights. *"Oh mon dieu!"* he cried out.

Sarah caught up to him, looked out the back window, and screamed when she saw Philippe lying on the ground in a puddle of blood.

The four officers entered the kitchen and had a brief,

intense discussion with Gabriel. One of them ran out the back door, dropped to the ground, and checked Philippe's vitals. Another spoke into his radio. The other two pulled their guns and began searching the house.

Sarah grabbed Gabriel's arm. "Tell me he's alive."

He looked at her but said nothing.

"No! That bastard. That *fucking bastard*!"

"Don't worry. We'll find whoever killed him."

She reined in her anguish. "It was Marcel. Come with me. I know where he is."

Sarah led him up the stairs and into her bedroom. She turned on the lights and pointed at the mutilated bathroom door. "He's in there."

Gabriel raised his gun, and she shook her head. "You don't need that." She led Gabriel into the bathroom and flipped the light switch. Marcel was lying face-up on the floor. His eyes were closed, his mouth slightly open. Blood oozed from a head wound.

"He's not dead. I drugged him."

Gabriel kneeled beside Marcel and removed the clip from his silver-plated handgun. He felt for a pulse and then frisked him for additional weapons.

Sarah gingerly pulled off her top, unpeeled the Velcro straps that secured her bulletproof vest, and let it drop to the floor. She stared in the bathroom mirror and saw two welts just below her bra. She turned toward Gabriel and pointed to her injuries. "That's where he shot me."

"Are you bleeding?" he asked.

"No. But it hurts like hell to breathe."

She looked down at Marcel and her blood boiled.

This oh-so-cultured gentleman had murdered Lisette and Philippe. And he'd shot her twice. Unable to control her rage, she raised her right foot and stomped him in the groin. His body jerked, but his expression didn't change. She raised her foot and stomped him a second time.

Gabriel looked up at her with wide eyes. "What are you doing?"

"I had to make sure he's not faking it."

Sarah stood in the Parmentiers' front yard and watched the ambulance drive away. No sirens. No blazing lights. No need to wake up everyone in Domont over Marcel's cracked skull and ruptured testicles.

After the ambulance disappeared from sight, she walked around the side of the house and observed the active crime scene. The area near the back door was cordoned off with yellow tape. Police technicians, wearing disposable white coveralls and booties, took photos and collected evidence while carefully avoiding Philippe's coagulated blood.

Gabriel saw her and came over. "How are you?"

"Not good. But at least I've calmed down a bit." She held up an empty glass. "This was full of cognac when Anne-Marie gave it to me."

"Why don't you get some sleep? Marcel's in custody, the house has been searched, and two police officers will guard you all night. You have nothing to fear."

"Okay. Maybe I'll give it a try."

She retraced her steps to the front yard, entered the house, and climbed the stairs to her bedroom.

chapter twenty-five

———

Sarah was awakened at 1:18 p.m. by a boisterous conversation in French. Curious, she got dressed and walked downstairs to investigate.

She entered the kitchen and saw René Vallon, Dan Spishock, and Gabriel Parmentier sitting around the table. They stopped talking and looked at her.

"I'm sorry," Gabriel said, switching to English. "I'm afraid we woke you up."

"It's okay. Is this a private meeting?"

"No, please join us."

Sarah sat down on the only unoccupied chair at the kitchen table, and Dan slid a half-filled plate of pastries and fresh fruit over to her. "Help yourself."

"Thanks." She picked up a ham and cheese croissant and took a bite.

"Would you like some coffee?" Gabriel asked.

"Yes, please. Black."

He poured a cup and handed it to her. "Were you able to get some sleep?"

"I think so. A couple of hours anyway," she replied and sipped coffee. "So, what can you tell me?"

"Well, we know that Erika DuBois, the woman from Paris who was arrested in Barbados, is a leader of *Patrie et Liberté*."

"The anti-immigrant group."

"Yes. And the man who confronted you at the beach is Marcel Joubert, a professional assassin from Austria. It looks like *Patrie et Liberté* hired him to acquire your drug."

"I got that. But how did they learn about T-3 in the first place? It must have been Paul."

"No doubt," Gabriel said. "We know that Paul wrote to that ethics committee warning them about your drug. One of their employees could have confiscated his email and sold it to *Patrie et Liberté*. Or maybe a hacker was trolling their computers and read it."

Sarah pursed her lips. "Big Pharma computers get breached all the time. Why an ethics committee?"

"For the same reason. To look for dirt."

"So, you think it's possible some hacker stole Paul's email and sold it?"

"Yes. Stealing and selling information is very common. And lucrative. His email to the ethics committee would have commanded a small fortune."

"Then they must have a ton of money," Sarah noted. "Paying for Paul's email. Hiring Marcel and his gang. Building a laboratory. This wasn't some cheap operation."

"You're right. *Patrie et Liberté* has wealthy backers.

And I'm sure they'd give generously if they thought T-3 could be a solution to the immigration problem."

"*Solution?* What do you mean by that? A twenty-first-century *final* solution?"

"Sarah, relax. We're a long way from a holocaust."

"I agree. But they *were* producing T-3."

"Yes. Fortunately, they didn't produce much of it."

"How do you know?"

"Because we took down their lab," Gabriel replied. "Everything burned to the ground."

Sarah's eyebrows shot upward. "So, you're sure you destroyed all the T-3."

"That's what I was told. And the two people working there were arrested."

"Good. What about Collin? Did you arrest him?"

"Not yet."

"How about the woman who was staying next to me at the hotel?"

"Unfortunately," René interjected, "she checked out before my officer got there."

Sarah turned to him. "I hope you can find her. I'm pretty sure she was going to kill me."

"I agree. Did you see the gift basket in your suite?"

"Yeah. Why?"

"It was not from the hotel. And it contained a bottle of *Santé naturelle.*"

Her jaw dropped.

"Oh, before I forget." He reached inside a suit jacket pocket and pulled out her driver's license. "I had to pay your hotel bill to get this."

"Thank you," she said and took her license back. "I'll make sure I reimburse you."

He shrugged. "It's okay. I used the money I found in your backpack. I hope you don't mind."

"Not at all. That was blood money."

Gabriel looked at his watch. "Any other questions?"

Sarah thought for a moment. "You're not going to let Marcel post bail, are you?"

"No," the interior minister replied. "He's a flight risk. And he's facing two counts of murder."

"Good."

"We first charged him with Philippe's murder. Then we searched his car and found the rifle that was used to kill Lisette Corbin."

"I knew he did it."

"And we've charged Erika with attempted murder."

Sarah took a sip of coffee and then lowered her head and stared at the floor. "So . . . as long as we're on the subject, what charges am I facing?"

"At this point, just assaulting a police officer. However, you also stabbed a man in California."

"It was self-defense."

"Possibly. But much worse, you created a drug that's wreaked a lot of havoc. There will certainly be additional charges."

Sarah slowly nodded her head.

"Of course, you conducted your experiment with the best of intentions. And you helped thwart a terrorist plot. Those facts will undoubtedly weigh in your favor.

So, who knows? We'll just have to see how everything plays out."

Sarah continued to stare at the floor.

"In the meantime, you'll be confined to jail. Once we've made more arrests and are confident you have no enemies lying in wait, you can post bail. Do you understand?"

"Yes."

"Anything else?"

"No."

"Then I must speak with you in private."

Gabriel led Sarah into the kitchen and through the back door. She stepped outside and looked at the ground. There was no trace of Philippe's blood. No crime scene tape. No indication whatsoever that a gruesome murder had taken place the previous night.

He turned around and faced her. "I have a very important question to ask you."

"Okay."

"What are the chances you could develop an antidote for T-3?"

"Zero," she replied without hesitation.

"Zero?"

"Correct. T-3 dephosphorylates synaptic cytoskeletal proteins."

"Meaning?"

"Meaning there's an irreversible degradation of the synapses. A person hit with T-3 may live for many years, but their brain will never recover."

"I see," Gabriel acknowledged. "And herein lies the problem. Your story will soon be breaking news. Millions of people will learn about T-3. So, the 'official' story is that an antidote has been developed. Someone overcome by it can expect a full recovery if they're given this antidote within eight hours."

"You mean . . . like receiving atropine after a sarin gas or Novichok attack?"

"Exactly."

"Except for one thing," Sarah noted. "It's not true."

"So?"

"So, you're going to spread a lie?"

"We have no choice. Do you want terrorists to realize there's no recovery from your drug?"

"No, of course not."

"For humanity's sake, it must be understood there's a cure for T-3. Only you, me, and a handful of others will know the truth. Is that clear?"

"Yes."

"Good. This must be our little secret. One we take to the grave."

———

Sarah climbed the stairs to her bedroom and surveyed the destruction. She remembered standing against a wall inside the darkened bathroom when the fusillade of bullets blasted through the hardwood door and sent splinters of wood flying in all directions. Her arms had trembled as she grasped the fireplace poker above her head. Her chest had heaved in and out. Whether she lived or died would be determined the moment Marcel burst through the door. Could she trick him one last time, or would he add her name to his list of "clever individuals" who thought they could outsmart him?

She snapped herself back to the present and took a deep breath. Marcel was in custody. He could not harm her.

Sarah walked into the bathroom, folded the police uniform and jacket, and tucked them inside a large shopping bag. She added the bulletproof vest, the pair of shiny black shoes, and René's reading glasses.

She put her toothbrush, toothpaste, and deodorant in the toiletry bag and zipped it shut.

An idea popped into her head, and her heart rate increased. Was it a crazy idea? Could she pull it off? She unzipped the toiletry bag, looked inside, and confirmed she still had a partially filled vial of T-3. It was more than enough to do the job. And nestled between her lip balm and a tube of moisturizer was a syringe.

chapter twenty-six

Sarah got into René's Mercedes-Benz coupe, and he drove away from the Parmentiers' home. She fastened her seatbelt and looked at him.

"I'm wondering if you could do me a favor."

"That all depends on what you want," he said as he turned left onto a two-lane road.

"Before you take me back to jail, I'd really like to see Marcel."

"Why?"

"To know he's not getting away."

René smirked. "I guarantee you he's not going anywhere. He was transferred to a high-security hospital in Paris."

"I believe you. But I still want to see him in custody. Otherwise, I'll keep having nightmares."

René didn't respond.

"Please. Just a quick visit."

He came to a stop at an intersection, looked both ways, and hit the gas. "I suppose."

"Thank you. And I don't want to be rude, but do you mind if I sleep?"

"No, not at all."

She tilted her seat back, knowing full well that sleep was out of the question. But rather than engage René in small talk, she wanted to focus on her predicament.

She closed her eyes and thought back to the day of her illicit experiment. At the time, she was hopeful it would lead to an Alzheimer's breakthrough. And yes, she embraced the possibility that she'd gain recognition. Ironically, her name would soon be known throughout the world. But for less noble reasons.

Would she face prison time? A lifetime ban from anything associated with neuroscience? Would Margaret and Neil shun her? And what about Rogelio? Would her actions—along with possible legal proceedings and the resultant media frenzy—drive him away?

She shifted in her seat and played over again that ghastly scene: René shaking Lisette, beseeching her to wake up. She'd watched in horror from the facing cell, knowing that no one could save the poor woman.

Then she thought about Philippe, the affable young man who'd whisked her away from Place Baudoyer. Who'd volunteered to guard her all night. Who'd made sure she had his phone number in case of an emergency. And who was murdered shortly after offering her a cigarette. She remembered the sickening image of him lying in his own blood and was overcome by guilt.

Sarah felt the car slow down. She opened her eyes as René was passing a slow-moving tractor. A tear trickled down her left cheek, and she wiped it away.

He looked at her. "Are you okay?"

"No."

"Is there anything I can do?"

"No."

Needing a mental break, she closed her eyes and imagined that all of the charges against her had been dropped. And that Neil, Margaret, and the rest of her coworkers had forgiven her. And that she and Rogelio had bought a house, were sharing weekends together, and had gotten engaged. Most important, she imagined that she'd put the horrific events behind her and was starting to enjoy life again.

She looked out the window and admired the French countryside. René rounded a bend and her eyes focused on a large grove of maple trees. Their burst of red, orange, and yellow leaves, complemented by spidery branches, brought back memories of her autumn vacation in Vermont. She relished this display of nature's beauty—a confluence of colors she'd never see back home in Redwood City.

Suddenly, all the resplendent maple leaves faded to blue. She gasped and opened her eyes.

René turned to her. "I think you just had a nightmare."

—

René parked his car in the restricted zone in front of Saint-Louis Hospital. He and Sarah got out and walked through the main entrance. René spoke to a woman at the admissions desk, and she pointed them in the right direction. They passed a gaggle of doctors, nurses, patients, and visitors and stepped inside an elevator. René pressed the number four. The stainless-steel doors closed, and Sarah looked down and tried to calm her nerves. A few seconds later, she heard a chime. The doors opened, and they got off. She saw two police officers sitting in chairs on opposite sides of a hospital room door and bit her lip.

René walked up to the officers, flashed his badge, and spoke to them. He turned to her. "Marcel's in this room. Are you ready to see him?"

"Yes."

"Don't worry. He cannot harm you. He's restrained to the bed."

"Good," she said. "Would it be okay if I go in there alone?"

René gave her a skeptical look.

"I won't touch him. It's just that . . . I need to face him by myself. To get over my fear."

He shrugged. "I suppose."

"Thanks."

Sarah hesitated, and then walked into the room. She saw Marcel lying in a hospital bed with a bandaged forehead and an IV and wires from various monitors attached to him. Shiny handcuffs secured his wrists and ankles to the bed frame.

She looked at him and slowly began to relax. He was no longer a suave hitman in a three-piece suit—just an old, unshaven man wearing a throwaway hospital gown.

Marcel saw her and his eyes bulged.

"That's right; it's me," she said.

Their eyes remained locked, and she remembered a similar experience at the California rest stop. She was in the back seat of a Camaro, and he was talking to a police officer. At the time, it seemed they had an unspoken truce. They would settle their score another day. And now, this was the day.

Sarah took four steps toward the bed. Marcel struggled to free his hands.

"Do you know a woman named Lisette? Hmm? Does that name ring a bell? She was a prostitute. You may have propositioned her a couple of times. Well, guess what? She's dead. You could say she died twice. First, she drank your bottle of *Santé naturelle*. Then you delivered the *coup de grâce*.

"But you weren't done yet. After that, you killed a man in Domont. A really nice man who was just trying to protect me. His name was Philippe.

"That's two innocent people you murdered in one night. So now you're going to spend the rest of your life in prison. And not at some 'Club Fed.' Oh, no. You're going to live in a little cage in some hellhole."

Marcel continued piercing her with his dark eyes.

She took another step forward and raised her right index finger. "Actually, that's not true. That's not going to happen. And do you know why? Because I'm going to do you a favor." She reached into a pocket of her cargo pants, pulled out a syringe, and removed the safety cap.

"Tell me, Marcel: would you like to take one last look

around this beautiful hospital room before I kill you?"

His eyes grew, but he didn't respond.

"No? Okay then."

She walked up to him, jabbed the needle into his left shoulder, and pushed the plunger. He winced but didn't cry out for help. She wasn't surprised. Marcel would consider it beneath his dignity to do so. He would rather die a proud man and forgo his lifetime prison sentence.

"It shouldn't be long now," she said as she removed the needle from his arm and backed away. He squeezed his eyes shut and began hyperventilating through his nose, as if being executed in a gas chamber. Just trying to get it over with. She listened to his rapid breathing and watched him twitch a few times.

"*Au revoir*, Marcel. *Au revoir.*"

His respiration gradually slowed down and became inaudible. After some time, he stopped twitching and lay perfectly still, his eyes closed. Sarah glanced at her watch, put the cap on the empty syringe, and slid it back into her pocket.

Marcel opened his eyes, looked at the monitors, and shot her an incredulous look.

"My bad. Tap water," she said and walked out of the room.

———

Sarah sat on the lower bunk bed, unnerved by her surroundings. She looked across the hallway at the empty cell Lisette had occupied and again replayed in her mind the events from the previous night—this time without shedding a tear.

The cellblock door creaked open, and she heard footsteps. René appeared and extended a piece of paper between the bars. "This is the phone number to reach your friend."

Sarah stood and took it from him. "What does he know?"

"Nothing," René replied.

"So, he knows nothing at all about T-3?"

"That's correct. But you can tell him. He's at a secure location in California."

"Thank you."

"Now, if you'll excuse me, I'll go back to my office and get you a lawyer."

"Can you get me a legitimate one this time?" she asked.

René glared at her for a moment and then smiled. "*Touché*," he said and walked away.

Sarah looked at the thirteen-digit phone number, written in blue ink on a scrap of paper, and took a calming breath. She pulled her phone from a back pocket, made the call, and began pacing the cement floor. Rogelio answered after the third ring. Her heart thumped.

"Hi," was all she could muster.

"*Sarah?*"

"Look, I know you're mad at me. And I—"

"You're *goddamn right* I'm mad at you."

"I can explain everything, okay?"

"Good. I can't wait," he replied with a mix of anger and sarcasm.

"First of all, I want you to know that I am so sorry for what I put you through," she said, her voice now quavering. "And I miss you, and I love you so much and—"

"Where are you?"

"What?"

"Where the *hell* are you?"

"I'm in Paris right now."

"*Paris?*"

"Yes, but I'm coming home soon."

"You're in deep shit, aren't you?"

Sarah was taken aback by his question and stopped pacing. "You're right. I am. I did something at work that got me into trouble and—"

"Is that why you just up and left me?"

Her eyes welled with tears, and she shook her head back and forth. "I did not leave you. I would never, *ever* do that."

"No? Then why did you write that note? And how did you wind up in Paris?"

"Please let me explain."

"Sure. And while you're at it, maybe you can explain why the FBI has me in protective custody."

"Rogelio, stop! *Listen* to me. That's why I called. I want you to know everything. And I want you to hear it from me. Before it's all over the news."

"*The news?* What did you do?"

Sarah inhaled and exhaled a deep breath. "You got an hour?"

"Yes."

"Good, because I have a story to tell you. A story about T-3."

"T-3?"

"That's right."

"*T-3?*"

"Yeah."

"Well, all I can say is, it better be good."

Sarah nodded. "Trust me; it'll blow your mind."

acknowledgments

I want to thank:

⌣ Stephanie Bookout. Friend and former coworker who enticed me to write a story. Without her, there would be no *Fade to Blue*.

⌣ Leslie Schwartz, Susan Snowden, Leslie Lehr, Jamee Longacre, Chelsea Robinson, Thornton Sully, and Greg Littlewood for their edits.

⌣ Derek Jeffers and Peter Anestos for help with French words and phrases.

⌣ Andrea Wasserman, Dr. Brian Cummings, Dr. Fady Hajal, Dr. William Jagust, and Dr. Bruce Hansen for providing medical expertise.

⌣ Ellen Haywood. After reading yet another version of *Fade to Blue*, she would give me some useful tips and beg me to hurry up and finish the damn thing.

⌣ Teri Rider and David Wogahn for their diligent work in getting my manuscript published and distributed.

275

about the author

H ank Scheer grew up in Minneapolis, Minnesota. He graduated from Central High School and attended 916 Vo-Tech Institute, where he studied machine repair and electronics.

He worked as a system repairman for twenty-two years at the USS-POSCO steel mill in Pittsburg, California, and was a member of United Steelworkers Local 1440.

After leaving the steel mill, he worked for ten years as an instrumentation tech at the Contra Costa Water District (IUOE Local 39).

Hank lives in Martinez, California, with his wife, Ellen Haywood, an I&E at a Pittsburg power plant. Now retired, he enjoys writing and recording music, biking, downhill skiing, world travel (fifty-four countries to date), and supporting working people fighting for a better world.